DOES CAROLE'S MOUNT HAVE
WHAT IT TAKES?

Carole turned Spice's head toward the woods. She couldn't shake the feeling that something was wrong, that Louise and Jessie were already somehow in trouble.

Willing though Spice was, Carole wished she were riding Jiminy, the sturdy Morgan, or Kismet, the stalwart Arabian. She hoped Spice had the courage, ability, and steadiness to do what she needed him to do. Still, he was the best horse she had. She had no choice but to take him.

She gave Spice a cluck and a kick to send him forward. They rode out into the darkness. The wind blew stiff and cold, and the snow was falling hard. . . .

THE SADDLE CLUB

PUREBRED

BONNIE BRYANT

A SKYLARK BOOK®
NEW YORK · TORONTO · LONDON · SYDNEY · AUCKLAND

RL 5, 009–012

PUREBRED

A Skylark Book / December 1994

Skylark Books is a registered trademark of Bantam Books,
a division of Bantam Doubleday Dell Publishing Group, Inc.
Registered in U.S. Patent and Trademark Office and elsewhere.

"The Saddle Club" is a trademark of Bonnie Bryant Hiller.
The Saddle Club design/logo, which consists of an inverted
U-shaped design, a riding crop, and a riding hat, is a
trademark of Bantam Books.

ISBN 0-553-48155-X

Published simultaneously in the United States and Canada

Bantam Books are published by Bantam Books, a division of Bantam Doubleday Dell Publishing Group, Inc. Its trademark, consisting of the words
"Bantam Books" and the portrayal of a rooster, is Registered in U.S. Patent
and Trademark Office and in other countries. Marca Registrada. Bantam
Books, 1540 Broadway, New York, New York 10036.

PRINTED IN THE UNITED STATES OF AMERICA

CWO   0 9 8 7 6 5 4 3 2 1

*I would like to express my special thanks
to Kimberly Brubaker Bradley
for her help in the writing of this book.*

CAROLE HANSON SHIVERED slightly as she hurried up the icy dirt driveway of Pine Hollow Stables. It was below freezing —cold for Virginia, even in mid-December—and the wind blew hollowly through the bare branches of the trees that lined the drive.

Carole looked at the trees and smiled to herself. She'd been thinking about trees all day, but not these kinds of trees. Ms. Kendall, Carole's social studies teacher, had assigned Carole's class a family-tree project for them to complete over Christmas vacation. "The holidays are a good time for this because most of you will be visiting your relatives," Ms. Kendall had said. "I want you to talk to them about this project. Learn from your own oral history."

Carole knew that oral history is history passed down as

stories from one generation to another. They had been studying it in school. Carole was excited about the project. Of course, she wasn't planning to spend Christmas with her relatives. Carole's dad was a Marine Corps colonel, and for years they had lived in different places all over the world. Now his assignment at Quantico, the Marine Corps base near Washington, D.C., seemed more or less permanent, but they had gotten out of the habit of spending the holidays with family. With the exception of her Dad's sister Joanne, who lived in Florida, and her aunt Elaine, who lived in North Carolina, she didn't know any of her relatives very well.

Carole shook her head to clear her thoughts. She'd had to stop at the library after school, and now she was running late for the riding lesson she took every Tuesday afternoon. It wasn't like Carole to be late for anything—even though she could be spacey sometimes—and it was especially not like her to be late for riding. Carole loved horses more than anything else in the world. When she grew up she planned to spend her life with them, somehow—rider, trainer, vet, horse breeder, she never could decide—but for now she spent every minute she could at Pine Hollow Stables with her horse, Starlight.

Carole rushed through the main door of the U-shaped stable and walked quickly down the aisle, calling greetings to the horses as she went. She swung her book bag off her shoulder as she hurried into the tack room. "Hello, Lisa, Hello, Stevie!" she said to her two best friends.

Lisa Atwood was already dressed in her neat riding clothes and was settling her hard hat over her medium-length light brown hair. "You're late," she said with a slightly worried smile. "Is anything wrong?" Lisa was a straight-A student and the most serious of the three.

"Library book," Carole answered briefly. She rummaged through the cubby where she kept her riding gear. "Overdue!" She shook out her old rust breeches and began to put them on. Max Regnery, the owner of Pine Hollow, absolutely hated it when his students were late.

"I can't imagine why you'd think a library book was so important," joked Stevie. "I don't worry about mine until they're months overdue. The last time, I ended up buying *Charlotte's Web* from the library—the book cost less than the fine."

Stephanie Lake—called Stevie by everyone except her mother—was equally good at riding and at getting into trouble. She was also usually pretty good at getting out of trouble, but no one had ever accused her of paying too much attention to books or to school. It wasn't that she wasn't smart. It was just that she could always think of more interesting ways to spend her time—like gluing her twin brother Alex's shoes to the floor.

"It *was* months overdue," Carole said. She pulled a sweatshirt on over the plaid blouse she'd worn to school and began brushing her black hair into a low ponytail. "I found it under my bed. And what were you doing with *Charlotte's Web*? I read that in the third grade."

"It *was* the third grade," Stevie replied, grinning. "My mom said I should stick with the school library after that. Fenton Hall doesn't charge fines."

"Not to interrupt," Lisa cut in, "but we don't want Carole to be late, and we certainly don't want all of us to be late. Carole, we've got Barq and No-Name ready. Why don't we groom Starlight for you?"

"That'd be great," Carole said gratefully. "I'll be there as soon as I get my boots on." Stevie and Lisa left the tack room.

I may not know much about my family, Carole thought, but at least I know a lot about my friends. She knew she could always count on Lisa and Stevie. The three of them were such good friends—and loved horses so much—that they had formed a club they called The Saddle Club. It had only two rules: Members had to be horse-crazy, and they had to be willing to help each other whenever help was needed. Those were the easiest two rules in the world for Carole, Lisa, and Stevie. And although there were other "out-of-town" members of The Saddle Club, including Stevie's boyfriend, Phil Marsten, the three girls were the only members who rode at Pine Hollow. They had had a lot of adventures and solved a lot of problems together.

* * *

AFTER THEIR LESSON, Carole gave Starlight a thorough grooming to make up for the hurried one he'd gotten before class. Starlight was Carole's pride and joy. He was a tall bay gelding with a lopsided, six-point white star on his forehead, and he had been a Christmas present from Carole's father. And from her mother, too, sort of . . . Carole's mother had died just a few years ago, and Starlight had been purchased with some money she had left for Carole. Starlight was still very young and Carole had been working hard training him. She was delighted with how far he'd come.

When she had finished and Starlight was happily munching hay in his stall, Carole went down to visit the newest horse at Pine Hollow—Stevie's mare, No-Name. Stevie's eyes were still glowing with the incredible joy of actually owning a real live horse, and she was brushing No-Name over and over even though the mare's chestnut coat already shone like a copper mirror. Lisa was standing on a step stool combing No-Name's mane.

No-Name wasn't really her name. That was the problem. The horse had arrived without a name, and Stevie wasn't going to be happy until she'd found the perfect one for her. No-Name was part Arabian, part saddlebred, and lately Stevie had been focusing on Arabian names.

"How about Sarouk?" Stevie was saying as Carole

5

walked over, picked up a comb, and began to work on No-Name's tail.

"No." Lisa shook her head.

"Tabriz?"

"Really, Stevie!" Carole said, laughing. "Where did you come up with those? Princess Jasmine was a better idea!"

"Ick." Lisa wrinkled her nose. "I don't think you've found it yet, Stevie. Not Sarouk, Tabriz, or Princess Jasmine."

Stevie looked a little embarrassed. "Actually," she confessed, "Sarouk and Tabriz are kinds of Oriental carpets. I looked them up in the dictionary."

"That's the problem," Lisa said. "You're looking at all these fancy names, and they don't fit your horse's personality. She's like you, Stevie. 'Sarouk' wouldn't fit you, either. Give her something straightforward—something adventuresome."

"But she ought to have an Arabian name," Stevie insisted. "She's part Arabian, and she should have a name that reflects her heritage. Bloodlines are very important in horses—and you know that Arab stallions can trace their breeding back hundreds of years."

"That's true, and I know that bloodlines can tell you a lot about a horse," said Carole. "I mean, good racehorses usually descend from good racehorses. Having a stallion like Man O'War or Secretariat in your horse's pedigree can really be important. And then look at show jumping: so many good jumpers are out of Good Twist's line, and—"

"Stop her!" Stevie cried.

All of them, even Carole, laughed. Carole was known for letting her enthusiasm get the best of her when she was talking about horses. They put down their brushes and began settling No-Name in her stall.

"But you're forgetting the other half of No-Name's pedigree," Lisa said, returning to the subject of names. "She's half saddlebred, and that was a breed developed in the American South. Maybe you should name her something southern, like Robert E. Lee—"

"She's a mare!" Stevie declared.

"Or Scarlett O'Hara . . ."

Stevie wrinkled her nose. "Frankly, my dear, I don't think so."

"That reminds me," said Carole. She told her friends about her assignment to trace her family tree. "I've decided to trace my mother's side," she said. "I don't know that much about her family, and I feel as if I should learn more. I want to remember my mother, and find out more about her life.

"Plus," she continued, with a teasing glance at her friends, "I'm sure I can find out something great about my family that'll explain why I'm such a fantastic person. There's bound to be someone special in my pedigree!"

"Like Man O'War," suggested Stevie.

"No, Good Twist," Lisa corrected her. "Carole prefers show jumping to racing."

They laughed again, and at the sound of their laughter Mrs. Reg, short for Regnery, came around the corner. She was Max's mother and the manager of the stable. She was known for her never-ending supply of horse stories, and also for her strange dislike of seeing riders stand idle when there was work to be done.

Now she smiled hello to the three girls and reached over the stall door to give No-Name a pat. "I was just noticing," she said, "that Prancer's stall needs cleaning out. If you girls don't have—"

"We'll do it, Mrs. Reg," Carole interrupted quickly. It was a Pine Hollow tradition that all the riders did stable chores. It kept the costs down and taught the riders a lot about horse care. They got a wheelbarrow and pitchforks and moved down to Prancer's stall.

"Prancer's bloodlines being what they are, you'd think she'd be smart enough to clean her own stall!" Stevie joked as she haltered the mare and hitched her to cross-ties in the aisle. She paused to pat Prancer as she did so. Prancer had been a racehorse until an injury made her unfit for the track. She was a Thoroughbred and still somewhat untrained, but she loved people and now she was rubbing her nose against Stevie's palm.

"That's the problem," Lisa said as she wheeled the wheelbarrow into the stall. "The fancier and finer the horse, the more it needs special care. In fact"—Lisa straightened up and grabbed a pitchfork—"we need to plan a celebration for Prancer!"

"Why?" asked Stevie. "Not that I mind a party, but . . ."

"Her birthday," Lisa explained. "New Year's Day!"

"That's right, I'd forgotten," Carole said. "All Thoroughbreds celebrate their official birthdays on New Year's. It makes it easier to sort them into age classes on the racetrack."

"And the poor horse who is born December thirty-first still turns one year old the next day," said Lisa. "That horse will never make it to the track. Imagine racing against three-year-olds when you're really barely two!"

"That's why most horses are born in the spring," Carole said.

"That, and the warmer weather. After all, most wild animals are born in the spring. But New Year's is still Prancer's birthday, and I think we should plan something special for that Saturday," said Lisa.

They all agreed that Prancer deserved a celebration. Stevie promised to try to come up with something. Lisa and Carole smiled—when it came to parties, Stevie could usually think of something good.

"Prancer—now, that's a good name for a horse," said Stevie as she carefully turned over the bedding in Prancer's stall. "Maybe I should name No-Name something like that."

"Like what?" asked Lisa.

"Like one of Santa's reindeer? Stevie, I don't think so," said Carole.

"It was just an idea," Stevie said a little defensively. "It's not that I actually want people to think reindeer when they see her." She paused. "How you think they say *reindeer* in Arabic, anyway?"

"Probably 'reindeer,'" said Lisa. "I don't think Arabic countries are famous for their reindeer populations." She grabbed the now-full wheelbarrow by its handles and began wheeling it down the aisle.

"Do you think you really need an Arabic name?" asked Carole. She unhooked Prancer's water bucket from her stall and carried it down the aisle.

When Lisa returned from dumping the old bedding into the manure spreader outside, she and Stevie began to refill the wheelbarrow with fresh sawdust bedding from the pile in the corner of the stable. Nearby, Carole rinsed, cleaned, and refilled Prancer's water bucket.

"I wouldn't call it necessary," said Lisa. "It's not that I dislike Arabic names. It's just that I don't know any that I do like. I don't know enough Arabic. And I think a name should mean something."

"*Barq* means 'lightning' in Arabic," Stevie reminded Lisa. Barq was an Arabian gelding that Lisa often rode.

"Veronica diAngelo's Arabian mare is named Garnet," Lisa retorted. Veronica diAngelo was a rich, spoiled girl that The Saddle Club knew and despised. Garnet was a beautiful horse, and they felt she didn't deserve such an obnoxious and uncaring owner.

"All that means is that Veronica is more interested in pricey jewels than in her horse," Stevie said. "Catch me naming No-Name after a gemstone. 'Sapphire, my precious Sapphire.' " She mimicked Veronica's high, whiny voice.

"Might as well call her Rolls-Royce or Mink Coat," agreed Carole. "It's not your style—and I'm glad it isn't!"

For a moment, Carole was lost in her own thoughts. Naming Starlight had been easy—she had first ridden him on Pine Hollow's annual Christmas Eve Starlight Ride, and, of course, he had a star on his forehead. Starlight was the perfect name. But No-Name was a bigger challenge. She wished she could help Stevie come up with a name for her horse.

The three girls returned to Prancer's stall and finished their work, and then put Prancer back in her stall.

"It's got to be a great name," Stevie insisted. She paused to give No-Name a final pat.

Lisa put an arm around her friend. "Don't worry, The Saddle Club will think of something," she reassured Stevie.

"We always do," Carole chimed in.

Stevie smiled at her friends, and they smiled back. Together, they could solve any problem.

DURING THE LONG bus ride home from Pine Hollow, Carole had plenty of time to think about her family-tree project. The more she thought, the more excited she became. This could be really fun! Carole couldn't wait to discover all the wonderful stories about her ancestors. Maybe her bloodlines *were* something special.

Her father was there to greet her when she got home. "Hi, honey," he said, kissing the top of her forehead. "How was school? And Starlight? And your lesson?"

Carole gave him a hug and took off her coat. "Have I got something important to tell you!" she said. She explained Ms. Kendall's project, and how they were to use oral history to learn about their own pasts. She told him how she thought that her past, which she knew so little

12

about, might be able to tell her something about what sort of person she was. Lastly, she explained why she had decided to concentrate on her mother's side of the family.

"It's not that I don't think your side is important, Dad—and Ms. Kendall did say we could do both—but I think I can do a better job if I just concentrate on one. Besides, your side is just Aunt Joanne and her family, and I already know them. Mom's family I hardly know at all. Minnesota's far away, but you won't mind a few long-distance calls, will you, Dad? Don't you think it's going to be great?"

Colonel Hanson smiled at his daughter's enthusiasm. "I think it sounds wonderful," he said. "It'll do you good to get to know your mother's family. Now why don't you go make us a salad to go with dinner." With a final pat on her shoulder he disappeared into his office, shutting the door behind him.

Carole felt a little deflated. She had expected her father to seem a little more excited—and she wasn't quite in the mood to wash vegetables. As she set to work, her mind was still on her family tree and all the relatives she wanted to call.

Her mother had had two sisters, one older, one younger, and one younger brother. Her older sister, Elaine, lived in North Carolina with her husband and three sons. Carole had been to visit them not too long ago. She really liked her aunt Elaine.

Most of the rest of her mother's relatives lived on a

Christmas-tree farm in Minnesota. Carole had never been there, and she hadn't seen any of those relatives for years. Her mother's brother, her uncle John, had a wife—Aunt Lily—and one daughter, Louise. Her mother's younger sister, Aunt Jessie, lived with them, as did her mother's grandmother, Carole's own great-grandmother, who was called Grand Alice.

Carole couldn't remember anything specific about John, Lily, or Louise, but she vaguely remembered Grand Alice as being incredibly old with bright eyes and a sharp, kind voice. And Aunt Jessie—there was something mysterious about Aunt Jessie, but Carole couldn't remember what it was. In fact, she couldn't even remember if she'd ever known what it was. Mysteries, she decided, would only make her project more interesting.

She rinsed the lettuce in cold water and began to make plans. Tonight she'd make a list of questions and call Aunt Elaine. This weekend, when the rates were lower, she'd call the Foley relatives in Minnesota. She'd probably need to spend a long time on the phone.

Her father came back into the kitchen with a big smile on his face. "We're all set," he announced.

"We are? About what?"

"The trip," Colonel Hanson replied. "It's on. Taken care of. Permission granted, Private!"

"Sir! Yes, sir!" Carole saluted. "Permission granted to do what, sir!"

14

Her father smiled, enjoying her confusion. "To go visit the family, of course," he said. "Isn't that what you wanted to do?"

"Fantastic!" Carole was thrilled. "Are we going back to North Carolina?"

"Guess again—Minnesota!"

"Wow!" Carole was flabbergasted. She never dreamed they'd be able to go all the way to Minnesota, just like that, just for her project. And what a project it would be!

"Remember?" her father said. "The Foleys have always wanted us to come visit them. I don't think you've seen any of them since your mother's funeral, and they told me then that they wanted to be sure to stay in touch with you. Besides, this is a great time for us to go. Work at the base will be slow for the next few weeks, and I've got some time off coming."

Over dinner Colonel Hanson went over the details of their trip. They would leave for Minnesota on the Tuesday after Christmas and stay until the next Monday, January second. They would be able to spend the New Year with the Foleys. "You'll have six days to talk to them," Colonel Hanson said. "Think that'll be plenty?"

"Six days to talk and listen," Carole replied. "It'll be more than plenty—this is going to be great!"

Colonel Hanson pulled out the atlas to show Carole where they were going. It would be a long and difficult trip, even though they would be able to fly most of the way. The

Foleys lived in the Arrowhead region of Minnesota—a remote, forested area in the northeastern corner. Nyberg, the small town where they lived, was halfway between Lake Superior and Ontario, Canada, and less than twenty miles from the Canadian border. "Lots of snow and wind and ice," Colonel Hanson said. "Travel can be difficult up there this time of year. But your aunts and uncle will know how to cope with the weather."

Carole hugged her arms around herself. She couldn't wait to go.

WHEN CAROLE TOLD Stevie and Lisa the news the next day at Pine Hollow, they were excited about her trip, but a little disappointed too.

"I wanted you to help me with No-Name," Stevie said. "But you can help me after you get back. Don't worry, we'll take good care of Starlight for you."

"We can feed Snowball too," Lisa offered. Snowball was Carole's jet-black cat, so named because she was so contrary. She always did the opposite of what she was told to do. Carole thanked her friends. She knew she wouldn't have to worry about Starlight and Snowball while she was gone—Stevie and Lisa would do everything for them that she would do.

"Do you have a name for No-Name yet?" Carole asked her friend.

Stevie groaned. "I can't think that hard during vacation," she said. "Perfection eludes me."

EARLY IN THE morning on the Tuesday after Christmas, Carole packed her bags. She still felt full of the warm feelings of Christmas.

On Christmas Eve she had ridden Starlight in another Starlight Ride, only this year she had had the sweet joy of seeing Stevie, flushed with pride and happiness, lead the procession aboard No-Name. Christmas Day had been great—another great Christmas with her dad. Carole found that even though she still missed her mother, especially around holidays, she had become used to and loved the quiet way she and her father celebrated. They had gone to an early morning church service at the base, then came home and built up a roaring fire before opening their gifts to one another.

Carole put her hand to her ear to be sure the earrings her dad had given her were still there. They were real gold, tiny horseshoes set with even tinier diamond chips. "For luck, not that you need luck," her father had explained. They were the first real grown-up present she had ever gotten from him, and she loved them.

And now, on this lucky day, they were going to Minnesota. Her father had told her a lot already, and from what he said she was even more excited.

"They should make an interesting project," he had said,

stretching out on the couch Christmas afternoon, while Carole played with Snowball in front of the fire. "The Foleys can trace their ancestry back to the days of slavery, right back to a slave in the Old South.

"I don't really know the details, but I remember hearing about a man who escaped from slavery just before the Civil War. He brought his family all the way to Minnesota and began to farm there. Foleys have lived in that area ever since."

Now, as Carole shoved a pair of jeans into her crowded suitcase, she remembered how the story had made her shiver. So this was her oral history. She was eager to learn more, especially since it sounded like she had a real hero in her family tree.

THE TRIP TO Minnesota seemed to take forever, but finally Carole and her father landed at a little regional airport in northeastern Minnesota. Carole ducked her head as she climbed out the plane's small hatchway. A gust of cold air hit her so strongly that she was nearly blown off her feet. With her mittened hand she grabbed the railing of the plane's steps and hung on. The air made her nose hairs crackle. She'd never felt anything that cold!

She and her father hurried to the terminal building. Inside, her father collected their luggage while Carole looked around for their relatives. A tall black man in a dark parka stood looking searchingly at the incoming passengers. Carole waved a tentative hand. "Uncle John?"

Instantly the man's face was wreathed in smiles. "Carole!" He came toward her and held out his arms. Carole held hers out to him, and he wrapped her in a giant bear hug. "How could I not have recognized you?" he said. "But you've grown—you're grown-up! It's been too long since I've seen you. Now, here, meet your cousin Louise."

Uncle John stepped back and Carole stood face-to-face with the one member of her mother's family that she'd never met. Louise was smaller than Carole and just a bit younger, but the family resemblance showed: She had the same high cheekbones Carole had, and the same sort of mouth. Carole opened her arms to give her cousin a hug.

Louise took a small step backward. "Nice to meet you," she said, with a polite smile and a little wave that prevented Carole from even shaking her hand. Carole was a little put off. Here was Uncle John, friendlier and more welcoming than she'd expected, and yet his daughter, whom Carole had been sure she'd like, hardly seemed glad to meet her.

She didn't have time to dwell on her thoughts, however. Her father arrived with their luggage, and after greeting him with a backslapping hug, Uncle John said that they had better get going. They had a long drive to Nyberg.

Outside the airport, the cold hit Carole even more strongly than before. The airport's electronic sign told her why: TEMPERATURE: −5.

"Is that a negative?" Carole asked, pointing.

"Sure, negative five," Uncle John agreed. "But you have

to take off another twenty degrees for the wind chill. When the sun goes down, it'll get pretty cold." Carole shivered harder at the thought. Colder than twenty-five degrees below zero? Stevie and Lisa should be here to feel this! she thought. She was glad that her father had insisted on her packing and wearing her warmest clothes. He had even found an old Marine Corps–issue cold-weather-gear parka for her. It was too big for her, but it was warm. Carole tightened the drawstring on the parka's hood.

Once inside Uncle John's four-wheel-drive vehicle and en route to the Foley farm—"the family compound," Uncle John called it—Carole began to ask questions. "Tell me about the family," she said.

"Well." Uncle John looked over his shoulder to give her a quick smile. "You've met me, and now Louise. Your aunt Lily, my devoted wife, is more of the same. You'll like her. And your aunt Jessie is my baby sister—she's thirty-four."

"She's the greatest!" Louise interrupted. "She takes pictures—photographs—and she sells them to magazines . . . oh, everywhere. All over the country. She's very talented, you know."

Carole was surprised by the way Louise seemed to come alive when talking about Aunt Jessie. "I remember hearing Mom talk about Aunt Jessie," she said. "Didn't she used to live in New York?"

There was a long pause.

"Well—" Uncle John began, but Louise jumped in

fiercely. "Don't talk to Aunt Jessie about New York. Carole, don't you ever talk to Aunt Jessie about New York."

Carole frowned. What could be so bad about New York? Carole had been there, and enjoyed the city. But she didn't say anything to Louise.

"The person you'll learn the most from is Grand Alice," Uncle John said, returning to the subject of family history. "Seems like she remembers all the stories for us. My father —that's your grandfather, Carole, and Grand Alice's son— he can tell a good tale too. But he and your grandmother go to Arizona for the winters now."

Carole nodded. She remembered her grandparents, though she hadn't seen them since her mother's funeral either. "If you need to talk to your grandpa, you can call him from Minnesota," Colonel Hanson added.

Carole looked out her window. The sun was lower in the sky by now, and the road was covered with hard-packed snow. Plowed snow was banked higher than Carole's head along the edges of the road. The wind blew gusts of frozen snow off the tops of the drifts, and shook the sides of the car. The land seemed dead. Even the trees looked cold.

"Maybe *we* should have gone to Arizona," Carole said. Everyone laughed, except Louise, who gave Carole a tight little smile.

"We haven't got too much planned for your stay," Uncle John said next. "To be honest, there isn't too much going on in Nyberg now that Christmas is over. We tend to hibernate through winter up here. There's a party on New Year's Eve—sort of tradition, our neighbors are hosting it this year—but that's about all." He looked back over his shoulder again and smiled at Carole. "Even if there's not much going on, I think we'll have a wonderful time," he said.

Carole nodded. She was beginning to be sure that she'd have a wonderful time whenever she was with Uncle John. She wished she could feel the same way about Louise.

Two hours later they drove up the main road of Nyberg. It was a tiny town, with a small collection of shops along that one main road and houses gathered tightly around the shops as if trying to keep warm. They stopped at the lone stoplight. Carole peered out the window.

"We're not there yet," Uncle John said. "We live in the suburbs." He laughed, then went on to explain that the family farm was ten miles on the other side of town. *"Waaay* out in the boonies," he said. "The farm is a sort of homestead, if you will—there are a lot of buildings. This way, we can all live together without getting too much on each other's nerves." He told Carole that the land, and some of the buildings, had been in the family for over a hundred years. "Years ago, we farmed wheat, but the soil is poor around here. My dad switched us over to Christmas trees. They do pretty well."

A few miles beyond Nyberg they turned off the state highway onto a road that gradually narrowed and then divided. Thick clumps of pine trees grew on either side of the road. The late afternoon sun cast long black tree-shadows across the road. Finally Uncle John turned onto a plowed dirt driveway and pulled to a stop in front of the largest of several white buildings. They were home.

The door of the house flew open. As Carole climbed out of the car, a huge, hairy, brown and white dog bounded across the snow, and leapt up to put his paws on Carole's shoulders. The dog aimed a slobbery lick at Carole's face. She ducked, laughing. "Who's this?" she asked.

"Ginger, *down!*" Louise said. "That's Ginger. He's my dog. Get down, Ginger!" The dog dropped his forepaws to the snow and Carole bent to pet him.

"Pretty boy," she said. "What kind of dog is he?"

"He's a mutt," said Louise. "I don't think he's any breed in particular. I found him when he was a puppy." Louise bent down to pet Ginger too. Ginger wagged his tail joyously and leapt up again, nearly knocking Carole down.

"Ginger!" A woman in the doorway called him back into the house. Carole grabbed her bag and followed.

"Carole!" Aunt Lily, like Uncle John, put her arms around Carole and hugged her hard. "It's so good to see you. We've missed you." She held Carole out at arms' length, looked at her closely, and hugged her again. "I know, you're thinking how could we miss you when we hardly even know you, but we could, Carole, and we did. Lord, you look just like your momma. Come see the rest of

24

the family." She gave Carole a little push into the living room, and turned to give Carole's father a bear hug too. "Oh, Mitch," Carole heard her murmur.

Grand Alice sat small and upright in a big flowered chair. Her hair was snow-white and her brown skin was creased into a thousand wrinkles.

"Hello," Carole said, suddenly feeling shy.

Grand Alice held out her hand. "Hello, Carole," she said simply. She took Carole's hand and patted it gently. Carole bent and quickly kissed her great-grandmother.

"So you're Carole," said a cool voice behind her. Carole turned. A tall, slim, and very pretty woman stood with one hand on her hip. The other hand held a camera. Her face reminded Carole of her mother's, but her manner did not. "You're Carole," the woman repeated.

"You're Aunt Jessie," Carole replied.

"That's right." She nodded once at Carole and once at Carole's father. "Glad you could come," she said. "I hate to greet and run, but I've got some developing to do." She held up the camera. "I'll see you all at dinner."

"I'll help you, Aunt Jessie," Louise said quickly, hurrying out of her coat.

"Louise, stay here," her mother commanded. Louise sank down onto the sofa, looking disappointed.

"You can help me tomorrow, Lou," Aunt Jessie said softly, and turned and walked down the hall.

Carole didn't want to let Louise bother her, but she couldn't help feeling a little unhappy. Louise was almost her age—they should be able to be friends. Why did Louise seem so eager to get away from her? And why had Aunt Jessie seemed so abrupt and unfriendly? Carole realized that she almost disliked Aunt Jessie, just on the basis of the way she'd said hello. That wasn't fair of her, she thought. It wasn't right. She vowed that she would try hard to like Aunt Jessie—she was sure that she could. After all, Jessie was her mother's sister. She and Carole ought to have a lot in common.

After a delicious dinner of ham and black-eyed peas, and piping hot corn bread, Aunt Lily declared a rest period before dessert was served. "Louise, why don't you show Carole around," she suggested.

Carole was eager to see the rest of the compound.

"There are six big buildings and a couple of sheds," Louise said as they pulled on their boots and coats. "Most of them are interconnected with covered walkways, but it's still cold in the walkways and we'll have to go out in the snow to get to the barn. You want to see the horses, don't you?"

"Oh, yes!"

"Main house first," Louise decided. She and Carole trooped down a long hallway. "The guest room you've seen. This is my bedroom, and this is my parents' room.

Here's the office, here's the bathroom, and this is the door to the basement." They went back up the long hallway, and Carole noticed that the walls were covered with framed photographs.

"Aunt Jessie took those," Louise explained. Carole stopped to look. The photographs were all different—some of farmland, some of lakes, some of busy city streets—even some, Carole noticed, of horses.

"They're nice," Carole said, touching one.

"She's very good," Louise agreed.

The tour continued through the rest of the interconnected buildings. There was a small house for her grandparents. "They still spend summers here," Louise explained.

Jessie had converted an old garage into a studio and darkroom, and attached to the back of it were two comfortable apartments—one for her, and one for Grand Alice. A big semidetached garage held farm equipment, and a smaller building contained Uncle John's workshop.

Carole's favorite building, of course, was the barn. It was small, but sturdily built and very old. "The timbers were cut by hand." Louise pointed to the solid wood beams that crisscrossed the hay loft. Carole nodded. Moose Hill, where she had gone to riding camp, had had a barn something like this one.

"These are the horses." Saying that, Louise's voice took on an affectionate tone, and she sounded more like one of

Carole's friends than she had so far. At least we have horses in common, Carole thought.

"This one's mine. His name is Jiminy Cricket."

Louise opened the first stall and stepped inside. Carole followed. Jiminy Cricket was a beautiful bay with an elegantly arched neck and long, flowing mane. He wore a thick plaid horse blanket securely buckled around his body.

"He's beautiful," Carole breathed. She held her palm out flat for Jiminy to smell, and wished she'd remembered to bring some horse treats. "He's the same color as my horse, Starlight."

"What kind of horse is Starlight?" asked Louise.

"He's a hunter—well, hunter-jumper; I want to make a jumper out of him some day."

"No, I mean what kind—Jiminy's a registered Morgan."

"Oh. Starlight's not registered anything. He's got a lot of Thoroughbred in him, and some Arabian, I think, and probably some quarter horse. He jumps very well, and he's agile, but he's not as lean and leggy as your typical Thoroughbred."

"Hmm." Louise looked distinctly unimpressed. She moved to the second stall. "This is Kismet, Aunt Jessie's mare. She's a purebred Arabian." Like Jiminy, Kismet was heavily blanketed. Carole admired her dainty face, and scratched her behind her ears.

"She loves that," Louise said. She waved her hand

28

toward the remaining stalls. "This one is Sugar and that one's called Spice."

"I know a horse named Spice," Carole said. "She's a Thoroughbred."

Louise laughed. "This Spice is no Thoroughbred. Have a look." Carole opened the stall door. Spice, indeed, was no Thoroughbred, but a massive bay workhorse, with great lumbering hooves and kind eyes. He wasn't wearing a blanket, and to Carole his shaggy winter coat looked as thick and rough as a polar bear's.

Louise patted Spice affectionately. "He and Sugar are just plain old mixed-breed part-draft workhorses," she said. "We actually still use them for chores, especially in the wintertime. They start a lot more reliably than the tractor."

Sugar, the mare, was like Spice but gray-haired. She poked her nose out of her stall door and Carole and Louise patted her too. "Nice horses," Carole said.

"Hmm."

Before they went back to the house, Louise checked the water in each horse's stall. "Sometimes the heaters give out, and the water freezes," she explained. "The horses have to eat so much hay to keep warm when it's this cold, that if they don't have water they can get colic really quickly. So we have to be careful to check. Usually the heaters are fine."

Carole was intrigued. "Heaters in the water buckets?"

Louise looked a little surprised. "Sure. I mean, otherwise we'd be hauling water all day. It only takes a few hours for an unheated bucket to freeze solid."

"It's a neat idea."

Louise shrugged. "To us, it's just normal."

They headed inside for dessert.

WHEN CAROLE AND Louise walked up to the main house, they saw a black snowmobile parked in the driveway. Louise brightened. "Christina's here," she said, and hurried for the door.

"Who?" Carole followed her.

"Christina. My friend. Come on."

Inside, Aunt Lily was dishing up apple cobbler and talking to a girl with short blond hair and blue-gray eyes.

The girl turned as they entered, and smiled. "Hey, Louise," she said. "I thought I'd come by."

"Hey," Louise said back. "This is my cousin Carole—remember, I told you she was coming. Carole, this is Christina Johnson. She lives down the road. We take the same bus to school."

31

"Hi," Carole said. Christina grinned. Carole was struck by the difference between her and Louise. Louise still seemed to be on her guard, but Christina's manner was openly welcoming—Carole liked Christina right from the start.

They sat down in the kitchen to eat the apple cobbler. Christina had been to Nyberg earlier that day and had seen some other friends of theirs in town. "Karalee, she got a Christmas present from John Harding—" she told Louise excitedly.

"No!" Louise said, her spoon halfway to her mouth.

"Yes! And she said—"

"Wait! What'd he give her?"

"I don't know. Earrings? Something like that . . ." Carole reached up to check on her own earrings. They were still there. "Anyway," Christina continued, "Karalee said—"

"You saw Karalee?"

"No, I saw Jen. But Jen saw Lauren, and Lauren saw Karalee, and Jen said that Lauren said that Karalee said that she thought John was really, really cute."

"Really?"

"Really. Better yet"—Christina leaned in toward both Louise and Carole—"Tim asked Jen to go with him!"

"What did she say?" asked Carole. She couldn't help but feel interested.

"She's thinking about it," said Christina. "They might

go to the movies this week, if Tim can get his mom to drive them."

"Wow." Louise leaned back in her chair. "I don't know why she just doesn't say yes. He's had a crush on her for forever. Do you have a boyfriend, Carole?"

"Sort of." Carole told them about Cam. "We don't get to see each other very often."

Aunt Lily, who had been out in the living room with the rest of the family, came back into the kitchen and smiled at them. She reached into the pantry, grabbed something off the shelf, and tossed it to Louise.

"Marshmallows!" said Louise. "What a great idea!" The three girls adjourned to the living room, where Grand Alice, Uncle John, Aunt Jessie, and Colonel Hanson sat talking in front of a big open fire. Louise produced some long-handled forks.

"The secret," said Aunt Jessie, taking a fork and bending low before the fire, "is to keep turning your marshmallow around and around over some nice red coals, to get it perfectly brown and even." Carole noticed that Louise turned hers around and around and made perfect marshmallows too. Carole had always preferred hers burnt. She thrust her marshmallow right into the fire.

"The secret," said Christina, laughing, "is to be able to get your marshmallow off the fork afterward!"

"If anyone knows that secret, tell me," Carole said ruefully. She pulled at the black and gooey mess she'd created, then gave it up and got another marshmallow to try for a more perfect one. The wind howled around the house and down the chimney. The fire flickered. "Brr!" Carole said, half to herself.

"Louise said you had a reason for visiting now, Carole," Christina said. "It's too bad you didn't come in summer. The weather's nice, and the lakes around here are so pretty."

Carole explained about her family-tree project. "It's not that I didn't want to visit before," she said, "but this was a good excuse at a good time, I guess, and Dad's being awfully nice about it." She smiled up at her father, who winked back.

"The project sounds interesting," Christina said.

"I think it will be. Dad was telling me part of a story about a man who escaped slavery and came here to Minnesota. . . ." Carole looked around the room, hoping that one of her relatives could fill her in on the details. Uncle John nodded and seemed about to speak.

"That rascal Jackson Foley!" Grand Alice exclaimed. Carole looked at her in shocked surprise. Grand Alice had been dozing off but now was sitting forward in her chair, her eyes snapping. "You want to hear about him, do you?" she asked. Carole nodded. "Well, it's a story, all right." Grand Alice leaned back, crossed her hands in her lap, and began to speak. Everyone listened.

"My late husband's great-grandfather was born into slavery on a cotton plantation in the middle of Georgia. No one knows quite where it was—ol' Jackson never told what his master's name had been, and when he got away from there he didn't bother to read the road signs on his way out. So we don't know who owned him—owned, Carole, think on that—or where it was he was born. Master gave him the name Jackson Washington.

"He had a wife. He had three little babies, born one after another, scarcely a year apart. Then one day he had a chance to escape. The Underground Railroad. A train, so to speak, had come for him." Grand Alice's voice had a musical lilt to it, and Carole was so absorbed in listening that she could hardly move. She knew about the Underground Railroad—the secret network that had helped slaves to freedom.

"I don't blame him for leaving," Grand Alice continued. "I don't blame him one bit. Think what it meant: freedom! The work he did would be his own—the money he earned, his own to spend. He could go where he pleased. He could name his own children, instead of having Master do it for him. And those children, growing up, could not be sold away from him. Freedom is a mighty and precious thing, but I don't think any of us, here in this room, can understand what it must have meant to a person who was born a slave. So I say, I don't blame ol' Jackson for leaving."

The fire cracked sharply. Carole jumped. Grand Alice paused, then went on. "His babies were too young to go—

too young to keep quiet during all those dark and dangerous nights of travel. His wife, they say, would not leave her
children. But Jackson, he had to go. He promised her that
he would come back for them, just as soon as he earned the
money to buy their freedom.

"Well, word came back to them by that same Underground Railroad. Jackson had made it safe to the North.
They heard he was in Boston. They heard he had a job,
and was working hard. Then they heard nothing. A few
years went by.

"The Civil War began. It became impossible to send
messages between the North and the South. Finally the
war ended, and the slaves were freed. Jackson Washington's family didn't know what to do. They didn't know
how to find him. They didn't know if he was dead or alive.
They thought he was dead, for sure. The children—two
boys and a girl—were now eight, nine, and ten years old.
With their mother, they set off north to find their daddy."

Grand Alice licked her dry lips. "Get me some water,
Louise, honey," she said. Louise ran to the kitchen and
came back with a tall glass. Grand Alice took several large
swallows. "That's better," she said. "So. They went to Boston and found that Jackson had been there, but had moved
on, so they moved on too. There were freedmen's societies
—blacks helping blacks find their families. Many families
had been split apart by slavery. With the societies' help,
that woman and those children tracked Jackson Washing-

ton from place to place. They looked for him for the better part of two years, working when they needed to, traveling when they could. They found him finally. I'm guessing that they wished they never did."

Carole felt the hairs on the back of her neck stand up. What had Jackson done?

"Jackson was working for a logging company in a tiny town in Minnesota, on the Great Northern Railway line near the Mississippi River. Name of the town was Foley. Jackson, never much liking the name Washington, had changed his name to Foley too.

"He'd given the name Foley to his wife. And to their four children."

There was dead silence in the room. Carole wasn't sure she understood. "But his wife and children were looking for him," she said.

"His first wife and children. His second wife and children were with him in Foley." Grand Alice sighed. "I don't blame him for leaving. I sure do blame him for never going back."

Aunt Jessie spoke. Her dark eyes were angry. "You see, Carole, slave marriages weren't legal. Legally, only Jackson Foley's second wife was actually married to him."

"But legally—what difference did legally mean?" Carole asked. She was horrified. "While they waited and waited for him, and tried so hard to find him, he'd just given them up?"

37

"He'd just given up," Grand Alice said. "Apparently, he'd decided that he'd never be able to afford to buy his first family's freedom, so he just started over. He didn't know the war would come, of course. He didn't know they'd all soon be free. But I say, he shouldn't have given up." She set her mouth in a firm line and folded and unfolded her hands.

"What happened next?" Christina asked.

"There was a ruckus that shook the streets of Foley. My husband's grandfather was the eldest of the second batch of children—he was five years old—and he can remember the women shouting back and forth and the children crying. Finally, Jackson's first wife and children renounced him and his lack of courage. They went back east to Boston. His second wife stayed on, but I don't know if she forgave him. They'd had four children together already." Grand Alice chuckled. "They never had another after that. But that's where we come from, all of us Foleys."

"What happened to the Washington family?" Carole asked.

"No one knows, honey. No one knows."

Everyone sat silently for a little while, thinking about the story Grand Alice had told, and then Christina rose.

"Thank you for the story," she said to Grand Alice. "Thank you for the cobbler and the marshmallows, Mrs. Foley. It's late. I have to go home."

Louise walked her to the door and Carole tagged along behind. They waved as Christina drove her snowmobile away. Louise yawned.

"I'm tired too," Carole admitted.

"I didn't say I was tired," Louise said a little crossly. She yawned again. "But I guess I am. I guess it's time for bed."

Carole was very ready to go to sleep. She gladly said good night to everyone in the living room, washed up, and crawled beneath the blankets of her bed in the guest room. She'd had a long day traveling and her family had given her a lot to think about.

She remembered Uncle John's kind welcome and the love and warmth that seemed to pour from Aunt Lily. She thought of Grand Alice's bright eyes, rich voice, and fascinating stories. Then she thought of Aunt Jessie, and the way she seemed to hold herself away from Carole, and Louise, who was friendly to Christina and Jessie but not to Carole. Worst of all, she thought about her own great-great-great-great grandfather, Jackson Washington/Foley, who had betrayed his own wife and children.

What kind of family is this? Carole thought. She had come here hoping—no, expecting—to find out great things about her past. The runaway slave in her background was supposed to have been a hero, not a traitor. The story of Jackson Foley surprised and upset her; she felt shocked and disappointed. Were all of her ancestors like him?

39

"There must have been plenty of good people too," she murmured to herself. Her mind was a whirl. There was no use keeping herself awake. Tomorrow she could learn more. She settled herself more firmly into her pillows and soon, the long day catching up with her, she fell asleep.

"SNOWBALL, COME HERE," Lisa called in what she hoped was a voice of authority. *Horses* listened to her when she spoke like that. She patted the kitchen floor beside her. Snowball looked at her, arched his back, and scampered away.

Stevie laughed. "See, I told you," she said.

Lisa sighed. "He doesn't change." It was Wednesday afternoon, the day after Carole left, and she and Stevie were in the Hansons' kitchen feeding Snowball and playing with him. Lisa tried again. "Snowball, go to Stevie," she commanded. Snowball came up to Lisa and leaned his head against her knee. "He was certainly well named," Lisa said, stroking his coal-black fur. "He's as opposite as he can be."

"I wish a name for No-Name would come as easily," Stevie commented.

Lisa smiled sympathetically. "We'll come up with something. I wonder how Carole's doing," she mused. "Too bad she missed the vacation Pony Club meeting. I thought all that stuff about bandages was really interesting, didn't you?"

"Yeah. I've wrapped most of them before, except for the tail bandage. But it always helps to go over things again." Stevie laughed. "And I don't think I quite got the hang of the tail bandage. Poor No-Name! Did you see the look she gave me, when I was fumbling around with her tail? What a mess!"

"But at least you can braid tails. Tail bandages don't do me any good—the braid's so bad there's no reason to try to protect it."

"Braiding takes practice," Stevie said, remembering her own messy first attempts.

"Remember how long it took you and Carole to teach me to braid Prancer's mane for the Briarwood show? It still looked like birds' nests—not that it mattered." Lisa frowned. At the Briarwood show Lisa had done everything wrong, and Prancer had been disqualified.

"It was a good learning experience, Lisa Atwood," Stevie said, imitating Max's deep voice.

Lisa grinned sheepishly. "That's for sure. Anyway, we've got to start planning Prancer's birthday—"

The phone rang, and Stevie jumped for it. Lisa grabbed

her friend's arm. "Stevie! That's the Hansons' phone! Don't answer it!"

Stevie shook her head. "Could be Carole," she said. "Or it could be Ed McMahon. Hello, Hanson residence."

On the other end of the line a girl's voice asked, "Carole?"

"I'm sorry, she isn't here right now," Stevie replied.

"Oh . . . could you please tell her that Karenna called? She'll remember me. We lived on the same base in California. My dad had to come here to Quantico for a few days, and he brought me with him so I could see Carole. Here's the number . . ." Karenna started to recite a phone number.

"Wait," Stevie interrupted. "Carole's not here. She's in Minnesota for the week, visiting relatives."

"Oh, no." Karenna sounded very disappointed. "I would have called her before I came, but I lost her phone number. I guess I should have called. Yuck. I don't know what I'll do this week if Carole's gone. Well, thanks anyway."

"Wait!" Stevie said. Since she answered Carole's phone, she felt as if she were a little bit responsible for the consequences. This Karenna was Carole's friend, and she would be lonely spending the week by herself. "Do you like horses?" Stevie asked.

"Do I? Sure! Carole and I used to take lessons together. I ride all the time."

"Why don't you come see Pine Hollow? That's the stable where we ride. I'm Stevie Lake, Carole's friend. Lisa Atwood and I could introduce you to Carole's horse, Starlight."

Karenna seemed a little surprised. "Okay," she said after a pause. "Okay, I guess I could. I'd love to see Carole's horse." They arranged to meet at Pine Hollow on Friday, and Stevie hung up the phone.

"I can't believe you just did that," Lisa said. "First you answer someone else's phone, then you invite someone else's friend, out of the blue, to come to Pine Hollow."

"She's not someone else's friend, she's Carole's friend. You know Carole would want us to be nice to her. Besides," said Stevie, grinning mischievously, "I *had* to answer the phone. It could have been Ed McMahon. We could have been the lucky winners of ten million dollars in the fantastic, fabulous sweepstakes giveaway. . . ."

Lisa had to laugh. At least part of what Stevie said made sense. They should be hospitable to Carole's friend.

JUST AFTER BREAKFAST in Minnesota, Louise and Aunt Jessie disappeared into Jessie's darkroom. Carole didn't mind. The night before, Christina had offered to take her on a snowmobile tour of the area today, and Carole had happily accepted.

The day was beautiful and the sun shone so brightly on the white snow that it made Carole's eyes ache. Once she was on the snowmobile the rest of her ached, too, from cold. Even though she'd worn a pair of Aunt Lily's wind-proof ski pants, her parka, boots, hat, scarf, and heavy gloves, the wind seemed to cut right through her. Still, she thought as she held on tightly to Christina, she wouldn't have missed this for anything.

The pine trees were laden with snow. Snowdrifts curved in and out around the trees, and Christina drove the snow-mobile right through them. They saw rabbits and deer tracks, a frozen waterfall, and hundreds and hundreds of trees. They also saw many more snowmobiles, most of them driving down the country roads.

"Are they out sight-seeing, like us?" she shouted to Christina above the engine's roar.

"What? No, they're probably going into town for some-thing. People use these for transportation around here, Carole. Cars and trucks get stuck in the snow. The wind's always blowing—the roads can drift shut pretty quickly."

Carole was impressed. She'd always thought of snowmo-biles as fun toys—like motorbikes, but for winter.

"Want to drive?" Christina offered.

"Yes!"

Christina stopped the snowmobile and switched places with Carole. She showed Carole how to start, stop, and turn, and Carole drove them back to the Foleys' farm.

"Thank you," Carole called, waving as Christina headed home. She herself headed for the kitchen. She thought she could smell lunch cooking, and she was hungry. Sure enough, her father stood by the stove stirring a pot of soup.

"Boy, does that smell good!" Carole plopped herself on a kitchen chair and began to unwrap her layers of clothing. "I had the best morning, Dad!"

"I can see that," her father replied. "Bright eyes, roses on your cheeks . . ."

"Roses from the cold. You can't believe how cold it is out there. And Christina says this isn't even cold, really, for this time of year—and it'll be like this until spring." Colonel Hanson ladled the soup into bowls and sat down next to her. Carole began to eat.

"What I really find interesting," she said, between mouthfuls, "is how everyone here arranges things differently because of the harsh weather—like the covered walkways between the houses. . . ."

Aunt Jessie and Louise came in from the darkroom and began washing up for lunch. Carole waved to them and continued. "And the snowmobiles, they're actually real transportation. We saw people driving to town to do their grocery shopping. Christina let me drive her snowmobile and I really liked it, but not as much as I'll like the ride this afternoon." Louise and Christina had promised to take her on another tour—on horseback, this time.

Aunt Jessie turned from the sink. "I'm sure to a delicate child like you, coming here from way down South is something of a novelty," she said with a slightly sarcastic sneer.

"You don't know even what winter is, or what it means to be up here in wilderness. Up here, the roads aren't always passable, and the phones don't always work. We have to take care of ourselves. You wouldn't know how to do that. You'd better let Louise take care of you on your ride."

There was a small silence. Carole said nothing, even though she felt stung by Jessie's rude words. She hadn't been raised here; she didn't know about winter, but she did know she could take care of herself.

What was Aunt Jessie's problem? Didn't she care that Carole was her niece, the daughter of her own sister?

You're just like Jackson Foley. He didn't care about his family either. Carole directed the angry thought at her aunt, and for a moment felt better. She wasn't rude enough to say it out loud, but she could think just as mean as Jessie could.

Then she had a second thought—if bloodlines were true, and Jessie was a rascal, what did that say about Carole herself? Here she was now, acting just like Jessie. She didn't feel better anymore.

She got up from the table and rinsed her bowl and spoon at the sink. She'd go riding. She wouldn't think about her family.

Carole dressed for the ride in clothing that Jessie and Louise loaned her.

"Your parka's fine," Louise said. "Forget breeches; they're too thin. Wear the snowpants Mom gave you this morning. And here"—she handed Carole a tube of soft knit fabric—"this is a gaiter." The gaiter slipped over Carole's head and fit snugly around her face and neck.

"A regular scarf could get caught on the saddle if you were thrown," Louise explained. "And the gaiter covers your face better, anyway." Next came a black padded cloth on an elastic band. Louise put it on Carole's head so that the padding covered both ears and the elastic encircled her forehead. "Like earmuffs, but you can still wear your riding helmet," Louise explained. Finally she gave Carole a pair of silk glove liners, a heavy insulated pair of riding gloves, and the strangest riding boots that Carole had ever seen.

They were black, knee-high, and had a foot shaped like a regular boot's, but the sides were made of thick, padded windproof cloth. "Insulated," said Louise. "Regular snow boots won't fit in a stirrup, but you'd freeze your feet in regular riding boots. Ready?"

Carole nodded. She was beginning to feel like a mummy.

Nothing, however, made her feel more normal than riding. The back of a horse—any horse—was where Carole always felt happiest, and riding Kismet, Jessie's spirited Arabian mare, was a particular joy. Kismet tossed her beautiful head and pranced through the snowdrifts. Beside her, Louise and Jiminy Cricket moved into a gorgeous, long-striding trot, while Christina and Spice followed her, and Ginger, Louise's dog, romped along behind.

Carole felt as if she were seeing everything new. Even though she and Christina had snowmobiled over some of the exact same land that morning, now with the horses she felt much closer to the peaceful, frozen wilderness. This must be how the early settlers felt, she thought.

"It's magnificent!" she shouted. She'd already learned that, with ears and mouths so heavily covered, she would have to yell in order to be heard.

"The best part's just ahead!" Louise replied.

They followed a cross-country ski track through a stand of tall white pines. Suddenly the track opened onto a beautiful snow-and-ice-covered lake, and they pulled their horses to a halt.

There was no beach, like Carole was used to seeing in Virginia. Instead, the forest ended abruptly in favor of large, snow-covered rocks, which just as abruptly ended at the edge of the lake. To their left a huge pile of rocks jutted dramatically into the sky high above the surface of the lake. Carole caught her breath—it was wild and spellbindingly beautiful.

Louise pulled her gaiter down to her chin. "That's Lover's Point," she said. "Sometimes in the summer we climb up there, but we won't try it today."

Carole understood. "With all the ice, it would really be scary."

Louise shrugged. "Aunt Jessie is going to go out there at

midnight during the next full moon. She's going to take a picture of the moon rising over the lake. She's not afraid."

"It's an awfully dangerous climb for a person," Carole said. She was surprised that Aunt Jessie would try it—not only in the winter, but alone and at night.

"She'll go by horse," Louise replied. "They're much more surefooted than people."

"That's even worse!" Carole exclaimed. "It might be true that horses are more surefooted, but Jessie would be putting her horse at a terrible risk! It's not right; the horse doesn't have a choice. The horse doesn't care about a picture."

"Jessie's horse will be fine." Louise frowned and pulled her gaiter back up over her nose. "Can't you tell she's a wonderful mount?"

"Jessie's always got the wildest ideas," Christina broke in before Carole could point out that Kismet's being a great horse had nothing to do with it. "Remember, Louise," Christina went on, "how she wanted to drive us to Louisiana last February? We had a three-day weekend and she wanted us to go down, dip our toes in the ocean, and drive straight back up. She said she knew where the Mississippi River started and she wanted to see where it ended up. She thought three days would be enough time." Christina gave Carole a reassuring look. "But we never went. It was just talk."

Still, Carole thought, driving to Louisiana and riding to

Lover's Point in twenty-five-below-zero-degree weather were two different things. And she didn't think Jessie had planned to ride a horse to Louisiana.

It was getting cold. They turned their horses and headed for home.

THE NEXT MORNING, after breakfast, Grand Alice invited
Carole to come to her apartment. "We'll have a cup of tea
and some talk," Grand Alice said.

Carole agreed to come at once, but as she followed
Grand Alice down the walkway to her apartment she
couldn't help but feel a little nervous. What other skele-
tons might Grand Alice pull out of the family closet? Carole didn't want to hear about another Jackson Foley.

Grand Alice's apartment immediately helped to set Carole's mind at ease. Sun streamed in from large windows set
in both the east and west walls of the open, spacious room.
Green plants grew on the west windowsill. A bright pieced
quilt covered Grand Alice's bed, a colorful rag rug covered
much of the floor, and gaily embroidered cushions deco-

rated the cozy red chintz davenport. The colors in the room were continued in a series of bright oil paintings hanging on the walls. Looking closely at a picture of blue and yellow wildflowers, Carole saw the name *Alice* in the corner.

"Did you paint this?" she asked Grand Alice, who was taking a steaming teakettle off of a little two-burner stove.

Grand Alice laughed and gestured toward the east window. An easel was set up next to a desk and chair. "Most mornings, when the light's coming in that window, I sit and paint, or I sit at my desk and write. The sunshine feels good."

Carole carefully examined the other paintings, including the one in progress on the easel. "They're really good," she said.

"They please me," Grand Alice replied. "That's all that matters."

Another wall was covered with photographs. Carole went over to look at them, and was astonished at how good they were. Some were landscapes and some were portraits, but an equal number were almost abstract. Her favorite was an extreme close-up of a row of icicles.

That's winter, she thought to herself. That's what winter feels like around here. Aloud she asked, "Are these . . ."

"Jessie's," Grand Alice finished for her. "Yes, they are." She brought the tea things to a low table by the davenport and continued. "There's more than one way of looking at everything. Some angles are more interesting than others, but some are just more confusing. When Jessie takes photographs, she goes hunting for different angles. Problem is, she sometimes does the same thing in her life." Grand Alice smiled. She sat down slowly, and motioned for Carole to come sit beside her.

Carole sat down. She wasn't sure what Grand Alice meant, but the way she was talking reminded Carole of Mrs. Reg, and her habit of telling lessons as stories. Carole was sure her great-grandmother could teach her a lot.

Grand Alice poured Carole a cup of tea, but at first did not take one herself. Instead she reached down slowly, and pulled a small wooden box out from under the table. "I got this ready for you when I heard you were coming," she said. She handed the box to Carole.

"I can't be sure what I'm telling you is true," she continued. "I can't be sure, nobody can, but this is the story that's been passed down, generation to generation, on my side of the family. My mother told me. Her mother told her. Way back, to at least the late eighteenth century, one woman told another. The story is that the first woman in my family came over from Africa on the slave boats and brought this with her, around her neck."

Carole opened the box. It was lined with yellowed satin. Inside was a small, finely carved wooden amulet on a leather thong. She held it up. It was a figure of a four-footed animal—a horse perhaps, or a donkey, or even a zebra. The wood was dark and smooth and the carving was exquisite. Carole held it up to the sunlight. She was amazed to think that something so delicate survived first a trip in a slave boat and then over two hundred years, passed down from hand to hand through Grand Alice's family until now, when she held it in her own hand. The little animal was unscathed, and the thought of its history nearly took her breath away.

"The leather's new," Grand Alice said. "Leather rots, you know, and the old string didn't look sound to me, so I had a new one put on. You don't want to put it on a metal chain, Carole, because it might scratch the wood." She took the necklace away from Carole and gently held it in her own hand.

"This would have been your mother's, Carole. I had only sons, you know, so I decided I would save this for a grand-daughter. I would have given it to your mother, but I waited too long. After she died, I decided to save it for you." Grand Alice slipped the necklace over Carole's head.

All at once Carole was overcome with joy and sadness. She flung her arms around her great-grandmother and buried her head against the older woman's shoulder to hide the tears that sprang to her eyes. She had never thought that anyone in her family, much less herself, would have such a treasure.

"I'll save it for special occasions," she promised. "And

I'll always remember the story. Oh, thank you, Grand Alice!"

Grand Alice patted Carole's arm. "You're welcome. I know you're a good person to give it to. You're like your mother, you know. Now drink your tea. I have pictures to show you."

Carole obediently drank her tea. But all she could think about was the amulet. "Just think," she said, fingering the tiny animal, "I may not be the first member of the family to be horse-crazy. Maybe she—the woman who first wore this —loved horses too."

Grand Alice chuckled. "Maybe so. And Carole, you take care of that necklace, but mind you do one other thing too. You be sure that you pass it on to your family someday."

Carole nodded solemnly, not trusting herself to speak. Someday she would give the necklace to another young girl, and tell her the story she had just been told.

After tea and two cookies apiece—"Always need a cookie with tea," Grand Alice declared, even though it was still close to breakfast time—Grand Alice instructed Carole to bring out several photo albums from the bottom drawer of her desk. Carole was thrilled at the number of pictures they contained. What stories they must hold! She got a pen and notebook ready so she could write everything down for her project.

First Grand Alice opened a big black album whose stiff cover crackled with age. "These are the old ones. There aren't too many of them—photographs were a rare luxury in those days. We start with Jackson Foley. Here he is."

Carole looked at his picture. To her surprise, Jackson Foley looked like an everyday person, not like the villain she thought him to be. He was thin and slightly stooped, and he looked a little stiff in his formal clothes, but he was smiling and his eyes looked kind.

"Course, he would have been Jackson Washington then," said Grand Alice. "On the back of the picture it says that it was taken in Boston in 1865, during the Civil War. It's the only picture of ol' Jackson I have. It may be the only one he ever had taken.

"Now here . . ." She turned the page and showed Carole another photograph, this one of an unsmiling young black woman in a frilly white dress. She held a baby, also dressed in white, on her lap, and a toddler leaned against her knee. Two other children stood beside her. The girl was dainty, with ribbons in her hair. The boy's belly pushed against his suspenders. He looked ready to fight. "This is Jackson's second wife, and their children. The boy, Frederick, was my husband's grandfather."

Carole wrote his name down. "Who are the rest?"

"The woman's name was Cleone. Little girl with the ribbons was named Elsie. She died the next year, but James —that was my husband, James—said his grandpa had been fond of Elsie and used to talk about her."

"What did she die of?"

"Oh, honey, nobody knows. In those days children could take sick one day and die the next, without anybody really knowing why. Weren't any immunizations or medicines—weren't hardly any doctors. Even when I was a child—I had a sister, you know."

"You did?" Carole tried to remember what she knew about Grand Alice's family. She didn't actually remember anything, brothers or sisters.

"I had two brothers and one sister, but all I remember of my sister is her casket"—she held her hands apart—"just this big. I was four years old and my whole arm swelled up from my shoulder to my fingertips, and no one knew why. The doctor came to operate on me, right on top of our kitchen table. He cut into my arm to drain the swelling. As I was lying on that table, just before he put me out with the ether, I looked into the other room and saw that little casket. That was my sister. She was two years old and her name was Sophie, and that's all I can remember of her."

Grand Alice pushed up the sleeve of her dress. "See here." Carole saw a thick, dark scar on the older woman's arm. "From the surgery," Grand Alice said.

"But how . . ." Carole was confused. "How can that happen, and how can people forget? I mean, your sister . . ." She didn't know how to say what she meant.

"People forget. Families forget. We're lucky, Carole, because our family told stories, and so we know an awful lot about our history. But that's why it's so important to keep

58

on telling the stories. Take little Sophie—I'm the last person left alive that ever saw her. My parents were poor. They couldn't afford photographs. They never had one taken of Sophie. I didn't have one taken of myself until I was seventeen." She shuffled through the old black album. "Here it is."

Carole smiled to see Grand Alice in a long ruffled dress, her hair piled intricately on top of her head. She was wearing thin, wire-rimmed glasses. "When did you start needing glasses?" she asked. Grand Alice wore them now; she needed them most of the time, but sometimes they hung around her neck on a thin silver chain.

At this, Grand Alice laughed long and hard. "Not until I was sixty years old and my eyes started to wear out," she said. "Carole, back then eyeglasses were the fashion. That pair just had pieces of glass."

Carole was more resolved than ever to pay close attention to her family history. These stories were important.

Grand Alice went through the rest of the old photos carefully, and Carole took voracious notes. The newer albums were filled with snapshots, and here Grand Alice sped up the pace. "When cameras got cheap enough that people all had their own, they took a lot more pictures. And let's be honest, some of them aren't all that interesting."

She hurried past old landscape shots from trips taken long ago, then slowed down again when she came to Carole's mother's childhood. "Here's your momma." There was Carole's mother as a baby lying naked on her changing table; sitting in her high chair with food all over her face and hair; wide-eyed with excitement in front of a flocked Christmas tree.

There she was again, playing with John and Elaine in the snow in front of the farmhouse—Carole was surprised to see that the house looked just the same—or, a little older now, running with her brother and sister along a rocky beach.

Then came a posed shot of the children together, a tiny baby lying across Elaine's lap. "That's Jessie," Carole guessed. In the pictures, the children grew up and graduated from high school and then college. John appeared in a football uniform, and Jessie as a gangly cross-country runner in a pale blue tracksuit.

Then there were pictures of Carole's mother and father together. Carole giggled. "I've never seen my father with that much hair."

Grand Alice nodded. "First thing the Marines did was shave it all off."

Then there was a picture Carole recognized from a copy they had at home: her parents together, holding an infant Carole.

Grand Alice turned the page of the album again, then very quickly flipped it forward to the next page. But Carole had already seen the picture: Jessie, perhaps ten years younger, standing with a huge smile on her face. A tall man stood with his arms around her, and in her arms Jessie held a young girl, two or three years old, with her hair in pigtails and a smile that matched Jessie's own. Carole even recognized where they were standing: in front of the Statue of Liberty, in New York City.

"But who was—" Carole started to say.

"We don't talk about that."

"But I thought—"

"We don't talk about that," Grand Alice repeated firmly. She continued on to the next page of the album.

Carole was puzzled and curious. Wasn't *all* of their history important? Was this another family skeleton? She wanted to ask, but something in the tilt of Grand Alice's chin warned her not to.

Who were that man and child?

"WHERE DO YOU think Karenna is?" asked Stevie. It was Friday afternoon and she and Lisa were at Pine Hollow, ready to ride. Barq and No-Name were groomed, tacked up, and ready to go as well.

"I'm sure she'll get here," Lisa replied. "I heard the directions you gave her, and for once they made sense." She flashed a grin at Stevie.

"I can usually make sense if I try. It's just that I'm usually not trying." Stevie ran her hand lightly down No-Name's velvety nose. "Horse," she said with exasperation. "Why don't you tell me your name?" No-Name blew gently into Stevie's hand.

"That was it," Lisa said. "She just told you. Too bad you couldn't understand."

A girl walked into the stable. "Are you Stevie and Lisa?" she asked. Stevie and Lisa turned around. "I'm Karenna Richards." She shook hands with both of them.

Lisa was a little surprised. She wasn't used to shaking hands with people her own age. Karenna, though, didn't look like someone Lisa's age. She was dressed in tight-fitting riding blue jeans and an elegant purple coat, and she wore dangling earrings and lots of lipstick and purple eyeshadow. Lisa had never worn eyeshadow in her life.

"It was nice of you to invite me to come," Karenna said. "Is this your horse?"

"No," Lisa said, "she's Stevie's."

"Her name is No-Name, but that's not really her name." Stevie explained her trouble with No-Name's name. Then she and Lisa took Karenna through the barn, introducing her to Starlight, Barq, and some of the other horses, as well as Max and Red O'Malley, the head stable hand.

Meg Durham and Betsy Cavanaugh were cleaning tack. They were better friends of snooty Veronica diAngelo's than they were of The Saddle Club, but they were Pony Club members and Stevie and Lisa liked them well enough.

"Hey," Stevie called to them. "Come meet one of Carole's old friends." She introduced them and Karenna shook their hands.

"Great to meet you," said Betsy. "Those are really cool earrings."

Karenna flipped her hair back so they could take a closer look. "You like them?" she asked.

"They're the greatest," Meg said enthusiastically. "Look, Stevie, they're little horse jumps!"

Stevie looked. "Very nice." She had never liked dangling earrings. Somehow she didn't feel that she was on quite the same wavelength as Karenna.

AFTER KARENNA TOLD Max about her riding experience and friendship with Carole, he allowed her to take Starlight on a trail ride with Stevie and Lisa. The girls were pleased to see that Karenna was indeed a very good rider.

"Do you have your own horse?" Stevie asked her. They headed for the trail that went through the woods and alongside the creek. It was the prettiest trail this time of year.

"No, I never have," Karenna replied. "I've taken lessons for a long time though. A lot of Marine bases have stables, and when they don't I can usually find one off-base nearby." She gave Starlight a pat. "He's a nice horse; I really like him. Carole's lucky."

Stevie grinned at No-Name's neck. She felt lucky too. "What's your opinion on the name issue?" she asked.

"What name issue?" Karenna looked puzzled.

"My name issue, remember? My horse doesn't have a name, and it's become quite an issue."

"I don't know," Karenna said. "I really don't. I guess I don't have an opinion."

"How about Magnolia?" suggested Lisa. "That sounds southern." To Karenna she explained, "No-Name is part saddlebred. That's a southern breed, so I think she should have a southern name."

"But she's part Arab too," Stevie said. "What's a magnolia, anyway? Sounds dippy to me."

"It's a tree, I think, or maybe a flower. What do you think, Karenna? Do you like it?" Lisa asked.

Karenna shrugged. "I don't know. It's okay."

They had reached the big rock that marked a bend in the creek. Lisa pointed it out to Karenna. "In the summer, we like to have picnics there. It's a good place to wade.

"Here's something you might be able to help us with," Lisa continued. "We're planning a birthday party for tomorrow for Prancer, one of the Thoroughbreds at Pine Hollow. Her official birthday is next week. We want to do something special, but we don't know what. Any ideas?"

Karenna shook her head.

"Maybe a carrot cake," suggested Stevie. "What do you think, Karenna?"

Karenna shrugged again. "Sounds nice," she said.

"Carrot cake because horses like carrots." Stevie felt like she ought to explain.

"Uh-huh. Sounds nice."

Stevie glanced at Lisa, who shrugged. Somehow, they

just didn't seem to be connecting with Karenna. Lisa tried again. "So, how long have you known Carole?" she asked.

"About six years," said Karenna. "We lived on the same base together for two years."

"Then you must know her pretty well," Lisa said.

"I do," Karenna agreed. "I'm not at all surprised that Carole finally has her own horse. She always was horse-crazy. And I'm sure she takes beautiful care of Starlight."

"Oh, she never forgets anything for Starlight," said Stevie. "For herself, though—that's another story. Lisa, remember the Mountain Trail Overnight a few years ago? Carole brought extra parts for every bridle, but almost forgot her own sleeping bag."

Both Lisa and Karenna laughed.

"That sounds like the Carole I know," Karenna said. "Once, I remember, she was reading a book on horse training right before an early morning riding class. She got so excited that she brought the book in to show our instructor. Only she'd forgotten to put on her riding boots, and she was still wearing her bedroom slippers!"

Stevie and Lisa appreciated the story. That sounded like the Carole they knew too. They traded Carole stories for the rest of the ride.

Afterward, while Karenna was untacking Starlight, Stevie went to Barq's stall for a hurried consultation with Lisa. "It's odd," she said. "We're such good friends with Carole, and Karenna's such good friends with Carole, that you'd think we would automatically be good friends with Karenna. But I don't know—it's not that I don't like Karenna, she seems nice enough, it's just . . ."

"I know." Lisa nodded. "She's not like Carole or like us. Still, I think we should be as nice to her as Carole would be, since she came all this way to see Carole."

"I agree. Why don't we invite her to tomorrow's Pony Club meeting? And maybe right now we could all go over to my house and call Carole, so she could talk to all three of us."

"That's a great idea. I'd love to hear how Carole's doing."

Karenna had brushed Starlight until he was clean and dry, and was putting his tack away. She seemed pleased to be invited to the Pony Club meeting. "I've heard a lot about Pony Clubs, but I've never been able to join one," she said. "I'd love to come to a meeting and see what they're like."

"We'll have the birthday party right after the meeting," said Stevie.

Karenna looked confused. "What birthday party?"

"Why, Prancer's," Lisa said. "Don't you remember?"

Before Karenna could respond, Meg and Betsy came up to them. "Karenna, we're going to go to the West End Mall for the rest of the afternoon. Want to come? Oh . . . Stevie, Lisa, you guys can come too."

"Great!" said Karenna. "I'd love to. Let me call my dad and brush my hair, and I'll be ready to go."

"No, thanks," said Stevie.

"No, thanks," echoed Lisa.

Meg and Betsy offered to show Karenna where the pay phone was.

"See you tomorrow!" Karenna said to Lisa and Stevie as she left with the other girls.

"Well, how do you like that!" said Lisa, a little miffed. "Now we can't call Carole!"

Stevie slipped her arm around her friend's shoulders. "We can't all three call Carole. But there's nothing to stop you and me from going home and calling her right now!"

IN MINNESOTA, CAROLE had spent a long, snowy afternoon playing board games with Louise. Grand Alice was sleeping, so Carole hadn't been able to hear any more family stories—not that she was all that eager to listen. Despite the good stories Grand Alice had told her, she was still bothered by the tale of Jackson Foley, and now she was worried about that photograph of Jessie too.

Then the phone rang, and it was Lisa and Stevie!

Carole was thrilled. "How is everything at Pine Hollow?" she asked. "How's Starlight? How is No-Name doing?"

"Great, great, and super-wonderful great," Stevie replied. "Listen, you'll never guess who went trail riding with

Lisa and me today. Your old friend Karenna Richards!" She told Carole about Karenna's visit.

"I sorry I missed her," Carole said. "But I'm glad you could spend time with her since I can't. How are you all getting along?"

"Just fine," cut in Lisa, who was on the second extension at Stevie's house. "But Karenna isn't here right now because she's gone to the mall with Betsy and Meg."

Carole laughed. "That's Karenna, all right. She really loves to shop. I'm not much of a shopper myself—but she sure is a good rider, isn't she?"

"She is that," Lisa agreed. They chatted a little bit more, and when Carole hung up she felt suddenly homesick for her friends and for Starlight.

"Something wrong?" asked Aunt Jessie, who had just come into the room.

"I guess I'm missing my horse," said Carole. "I'm used to seeing him every day. He's a really great horse, you know—he's got lots of talent and can really jump, but he's also sweet and affectionate. I really love him."

"I'm sure any girl would think her own horse was special," said Aunt Jessie, not seeming very impressed. "But honestly, I can't see how any horse that's just used for fun riding and that fancy show stuff can be much of a real horse."

Carole was offended. "Show riding is a lot harder than

regular riding," she said. "It requires knowledge, strength, and discipline. I might not have done too much of it, but I did get a blue ribbon at a show on Long Island and I was Reserve Champion at Briarwood." Carole felt defensive about her riding skills for the first time in her memory. Usually everyone knew that she was a good rider. "Of course," she continued, "neither of those shows was quite as important as the American Horse Show that I went to in New York, but some day I'm going to . . ."

Jessie flinched when Carole said the words *New York*. Carole remembered the picture of Jessie at the Statue of Liberty. "Did you go to the American when you were in New York?" she asked.

"No, I never went there." Jessie twisted her hands together and for a moment looked confused. Then she looked angry. "I never was in New York," she said. "That part of my life is dead. Gone. Over!" She ran from the room.

"What did I say?" Carole asked Louise. She was astonished at Jessie's reaction to her simple question.

"I told you not to talk about New York in front of Aunt Jessie," Louise said harshly. Looking worried, she ran after her aunt.

Carole sat back down, feeling embarrassed. She hadn't meant to upset Aunt Jessie, but she couldn't imagine why the mere mention of the words *New York* was enough to set her off like that. Then she remembered the man and child with Jessie in the picture. Could they be Jessie's husband and daughter? Could Jessie have abandoned them in New York?

Just like Jackson Foley had abandoned his family?

AT THE UNMOUNTED Horse Wise meeting at Pine Hollow the next day, Karenna showed up with Betsy and Meg just as Max called the room to order. She waved to Stevie and Lisa, but she sat down with Betsy and Meg, and she seemed to be having a great time. The three of them whispered and giggled throughout May Grover's entire presentation on winter stable management.

Finally the girls' chattering attracted Max's attention. "Meg, do you and Betsy have something you wish to share with the group?" he asked in a stern voice. He didn't single out Karenna, but his glare included her. Max hated it when students talked during lessons or Horse Wise meetings. May looked indignant too.

"No, no, I don't think I do," said Meg. Stevie thought

Meg looked as if she were having trouble keeping a straight face. She wondered what the joke was.

"Perhaps you and Betsy can present a topic at our next meeting," Max suggested. "Let's see . . . Stall Cleaning and its Role in Parasite Control." He wrote it down in his pocket calendar. "January thirteenth, okay?"

This time Meg barely suppressed her groan. "Uh, sure, Max," she mumbled. "Sorry if we bothered you, May." They quieted down, but a few minutes later Stevie saw them giggling again.

"I wonder what's so funny," she whispered to Lisa.

"I don't know, but I wish I knew," Lisa answered. "It doesn't seem right that Karenna is spending so much time with Meg and Betsy, does it?"

Stevie shook her head. "If she's Carole's friend, she ought to be sitting with us. If she's got a good joke to tell, she should be telling it to us."

Lisa agreed, but figured they could ask Karenna about it after the Pony Club meeting, when they all met for Prancer's birthday party.

When the meeting was over, however, she couldn't find Karenna anywhere. Lisa had stepped into the locker room for a moment and when she came out Karenna was gone. Exasperated, she gave up and went to meet Stevie outside Prancer's stall.

They had not managed to come up with a very interesting plan for the birthday party—even Stevie's famous brain had had to admit defeat. The carrot cake idea had failed, because neither of their mothers would let them attempt to make one, and the cakes in the bakery cost too much. Instead, they had just brought a lot of apples, carrots, and other treats to give to the Thoroughbreds.

"That's an *awful* lot of carrots," Lisa said as she sat down on a hay bale next to Stevie. "Do you think Prancer can eat that many?"

Stevie grinned. "The ten-pound bags were on sale. Besides, I think Prancer would say that there's no such thing as too many carrots."

Lisa agreed. "I couldn't find Karenna. We'll just have to wait for her."

They waited and waited. Finally Karenna ran up to them breathless, with Meg and Betsy in tow. "We're going on a trail ride; Max said we could," she said. "Do you two want to come?"

"I don't think so," Lisa said indignantly. "We've got Prancer's—"

"No, thank you," Stevie cut in. She gave Lisa a warning look and Lisa understood and was quiet. If Karenna had forgotten about the party, they weren't going to remind her.

Karenna shrugged. "Okay. Guess I'll see you later. Anyway, it was nice meeting you guys. Tell Carole I said hi, okay? Tell her I'm sorry she wasn't here."

"We will," Lisa promised. "I know she was sorry not to

see you." She watched as Karenna followed Meg and Betsy into the tack room. "She did forget about the party," Lisa said.

"Then we'll do just as well without her," said Stevie. "No use trying to make her stay." As she spoke, Karenna came out of the tack room carrying Carole's saddle and bridle. She disappeared into Starlight's stall.

Lisa stared. "She's not riding Starlight, is she?" She couldn't believe that Karenna would do such a thing without telling them!

"Max must have said she could." Stevie sounded doubtful. "He said they could go on the trail ride, and he would have told them which horses to take. Besides, Karenna's not foolish. She wouldn't take Starlight out without Max's permission."

"I don't know if we should let her," Lisa argued. "We're supposed to be taking care of Starlight. If anything happens to him it'll be our fault."

"On the other hand," Stevie argued back, "she is Carole's friend, and we know she's a good rider. I agree with what you think, but Max must have said it was okay."

"Yeah." Lisa paused. "I still don't like it."

"Me either," Stevie sighed. "I guess it's time to start the party, not that it feels like much of a party. The problem is, since Karenna is Carole's friend, we've been hoping she would be like Carole, and she's not. What we need, really, is Carole herself."

Lisa nodded. There was nothing she could say to that. They opened Prancer's stall door, and the beautiful mare came toward them, her ears pricked forward. She always seemed glad to see the girls.

"Happy Birthday to you," they began to sing.

When they were finished, Lisa offered the Thoroughbred a carrot, and Stevie gave her an enthusiastic hug. Prancer ate the carrot delicately. Then Stevie gave her an apple, which she ate in several bites, and Lisa put her arms around the mare's neck.

"Happy Birthday, you beautiful darling," Lisa murmured into Prancer's ear. She had always loved Prancer, and she hoped to ride her well—and in horse shows—someday. Lisa knew that both she and Prancer needed a little more training before that would be possible. Green horses and green riders were always a bad combination. Prancer had been a racehorse only a short time ago, and Lisa, though she rode a great deal now, had not been doing it very long and her relative inexperience sometimes showed. Still, Lisa felt they would make a good team when they were both ready. "In a year or two, darling," she promised Prancer, and hugged her again.

They moved down the aisle to Topside, the champion Thoroughbred that Stevie had always ridden until she got No-Name a few weeks ago. They sang "Happy Birthday" to Topside, and offered him treats and hugs.

"Do you think he misses me?" Stevie asked. She rubbed

his neck affectionately. "He's a great horse, and he taught me a lot about riding. I do miss him, but I'd rather be riding my own horse than any other horse in the world."

Lisa nodded. Though she didn't have her own horse, she could imagine how it must feel. "I'm sure he's fine," she said to Stevie. "He might miss you, but other people have always ridden him, too, and soon Max will find someone like you to ride him most of the time. He didn't seem to miss Dorothy too much when he first got here, did he?" Dorothy DeSoto, a former championship rider, had owned and ridden Topside until an accident had ended her competitive career. Dorothy was a great friend to all the girls.

"He didn't seem unhappy. He's always seemed to like Pine Hollow."

"He's still at Pine Hollow, so he should still be happy. Don't worry, Stevie. I'm sure Dorothy didn't worry when she sold Topside to Max. Besides, you can come visit him whenever you want. All you have to do is walk down the aisle."

"True," Stevie said, brightening. "Good boy, Topside." With another pat to his sleek brown neck, she closed his stall and they went on to the next Thoroughbred.

They were singing to their sixth Thoroughbred, a leggy mare named Calypso, when they noticed that they had attracted the attention of all the other horses in the barn. The smell of fresh-chewed carrots and apples had every single horse in Pine Hollow hanging its head over the open part of its stall door, and when Lisa and Stevie looked around, the horses, from the tiny pony Penny to the giant half-Percheron Cocoa, started whickering in chorus.

Lisa and Stevie looked down each aisle, then at each other, and laughed.

"We've started something," Lisa said. "They all think that they're going to get carrots. They don't realize that it's only the Thoroughbreds' birthday."

"Well, there's only one logical solution," Stevie said cheerfully.

"After all," Lisa agreed, "it's not really fair to leave out the rest of the horses just because they aren't Thoroughbreds."

"Therefore," Stevie concluded, "as two thirds of the members of The Saddle Club, we henceforth declare today to be the official birthday of all the horses in Pine Hollow. Saddle Club birthday treatment for all!"

"Hear, hear!" Lisa waved a carrot in the air in confirmation. "Good thing you brought too many carrots, Stevie."

"Too many? I brought *enough*."

It took a long time to sing "Happy Birthday" to every single horse at Pine Hollow, but the girls made sure that they did a thorough job and gave every horse lots of attention. They all were good horses and they all deserved to be fussed over.

"Why didn't we think of this before?" asked Stevie. She

wiped carrot slobber off the sleeve of her jacket. Cocoa had thanked her with a messy nudge.

"I don't know, but we'll definitely have to think of it again. I declare this to be a new Pine Hollow tradition— New Year's birthday celebrations!"

"A new Saddle Club tradition," Stevie corrected her.

Lisa grinned. "A new Saddle Club tradition at Pine Hollow," she said.

They had just finished the last horse when Lisa's mom arrived to take them home. Stevie was spending the night at Lisa's house, and since it was New Year's Eve they had decided to stay up as late as they could. Lisa's mom and dad were going to a party, so Lisa and Stevie had the VCR all to themselves. They'd rented *National Velvet*, *International Velvet*, *Phar Lap*, and *The Black Stallion*.

"Horses and popcorn until dawn," Stevie said enthusiastically.

"Maybe brownies too," said Lisa. "Horses and popcorn and brownies—perfect."

As they were getting into the car, Stevie pointed toward the woods. "Look." Meg, Betsy, and Karenna were just returning to Pine Hollow. "They sure took a long enough ride."

"And poor Starlight didn't get his birthday treats," said Lisa. She waved at the girls, but they were too far away to notice her. "At least Starlight looks okay. Nothing happened to him."

"If we had really thought something would happen to him we wouldn't have let Karenna ride him. We'll give Starlight his treats tomorrow," said Stevie. "I'm glad Carole is coming home soon."

"So am I," said Lisa. "The Saddle Club isn't The Saddle Club without her."

9

THAT NIGHT THE Foleys went to the New Year's Eve party at Christina's house. The party had been a neighborhood tradition for many years, and since traditions were an important part of family history, Carole brought her notebook with her to take notes.

Christina's parents, the Johnsons, were the Foleys' nearest neighbors, but they lived nearly four miles away. The night was bitterly cold—even Carole, who had thought that every night in Minnesota was bitterly cold, could recognize an extra piercing quality to the air—and the sky was crystal clear. More stars were shining than Carole had ever seen. Uncle John explained to her that clouds acted like a blanket to keep the earth warm. Clear nights were always the coldest.

81

The cold didn't keep anyone home, however. Even Grand Alice bundled up and came along, and from the number of four-wheel drives and snowmobiles parked in the driveway, Carole guessed that most of the town of Nyberg was celebrating with them.

They entered the house by a lean-to off the kitchen. The large country kitchen was bright and warm, and full of good smells.

Christina came running to greet them. "We'll put your coats upstairs," she said, gathering them as the Foleys took them off. "Most of the guests are in the living room right now. Food is on the buffet in the dining room, drinks are here in the kitchen, and dancing starts soon in the family room. If you need anything, just ask. And Louise, Emile's coming!" Christina dashed upstairs with her arms full of coats.

"Who's Emile?" asked Carole.

"Her boyfriend," said Louise. "He's French-Canadian. He plays hockey for the high school."

While Uncle John and Aunt Lily greeted friends and introduced Colonel Hanson to them, Carole took out her notebook and made a few notes.

There's lots of food. Everyone pitched in and brought something to share. Aunt Lily brought two pumpkin pies made from pumpkins she grew herself. Grand Alice made cookies, the same kind she gave me with tea. The house is warm and crowded, and everyone seems happy. There are about twenty people here so far—whoops, twenty-three, three more just came in—and they are laughing and shouting hello. Christina's dad just put some great jazz on the stereo. It's a nice party, and it's good to know that my family has so many friends.

Carole closed her notebook. She was finished writing; it was time to have fun.

The door opened. Aunt Jessie blew in with a whirl of frigid air. She had driven over separately because she had said she wanted to finish developing some pictures first, but she had finished pretty quickly. Carole watched her aunt take off her coat, greet a few friends, and help herself to some food. Then, to her surprise, Jessie walked over to her and smiled. "Happy New Year, Carole," she said. "Are you having fun?"

"Sure," Carole replied. "Everyone here has been super nice." She meant it; she felt very comfortable in Christina's home.

Aunt Jessie smiled again, a small but not unfriendly smile. "Everyone's been nice to you except maybe me. I thought I should make a small apology. I know that I haven't been as friendly as I should have been. After all, you are my niece, and I do want to get to know you better. Also, I want to say that I didn't mean to belittle your horse or your knowledge of horses. Sometimes I've got a real attitude. I'm sorry, okay?" Aunt Jessie held out her hand to Carole.

"Okay." Carole shook hands gladly. She still felt a bit strange toward Jessie—it seemed like every time she talked to her, Jessie was angry about something—but she was happy to be on better terms with her. "People can tease me about almost anything, you know—except horses," she added. "I can be a little sensitive sometimes."

Aunt Jessie smiled. "I feel the same way about my photography. You and I have something in common." She offered Carole one of the chocolate chip cookies from her plate.

Christina brought over Emile—a short, good-looking boy with black hair and uneven eyebrows—and introduced him to Carole.

"Yo," Emile said, nodding at Carole and hooking his thumbs into the belt loops of his jeans.

"Yo," Carole said back, imitating his nod and hooking her own thumbs into her jeans. Aunt Jessie laughed out loud, winked at Carole, and sauntered off toward the rest of the party.

"What is this music?" Christina exclaimed with mock horror. "My dad's lousy jazz. He's always sneaking this stuff onto the stereo. Let's put on something we can dance to." She switched the music to something with a faster beat, grabbed Emile with one hand and Carole with the other, and hauled them both into the family room, where the furniture had been moved to clear space for dancing. Carole was all for it. She loved to dance. Before long, most of the party-goers had joined them on the dance floor.

Three songs later, when she stopped to catch her breath, she saw Aunt Jessie standing across the room. Jessie was staring out the uncurtained window at a full moon with bare black branches silhouetted against it. Something about the way she stood with the moonlight falling against her face reminded Carole suddenly of her own mother, whom she still missed very much. Carole couldn't forget the bad things she suspected about Aunt Jessie's past, but she was glad that they'd cleared some of the air between them. Carole's mother had loved her sister Jessie.

Carole walked over to Aunt Jessie. "Hello," she said softly.

Aunt Jessie turned to her with an excited smile on her face. "Oh, Carole, this is just the kind of night I need to ride Kismet over to Lover's Point to take my pictures."

Carole was sure she didn't mean it, but she was horrified that Aunt Jessie would even talk about doing something so foolish. "You'd have to be crazy to consider taking your horse out on a night like this," she said. "You'd endanger her life, riding up there!" Aunt Jessie didn't reply. "You'd have to be crazy," Carole repeated, shaking her head.

"Well, that's what you think anyway, isn't it?" Aunt Jessie replied, anger seeping back into her tone. "You think I'm crazy, don't you?"

"No," Carole answered. "But I think it would be a pretty bad decision to go out."

"I make my own decisions," Aunt Jessie snapped. She crossed her arms angrily; her dark eyes were blazing. "I don't need you to tell me how or when to ride my horse. I don't need you—or anyone else—to decide what I do."

Goaded by her aunt's tone, Carole felt herself growing angry too—more angry than she thought she would be. Every rude word Jessie had said, and everything that Carole suspected, came back to her now, and she spat out, "I don't think you've been making very good decisions with your life so far. This one might be minor compared to some of the other colossal bloopers you've made, but it would be dangerous for Kismet as well as for you. It's stupid and reckless, and I think you should know better."

Jessie drew herself up tall. "And I think I don't care what you think!" she shouted. She stormed out of the room.

Carole, watching her go, was struck again by how much Jessie looked like Carole's mother. But her mother hadn't acted like Jessie at all.

Louise came up to Carole and glared at her reproachfully. "What did you say to her?" she demanded. "Why did you get her so upset?"

"I'm sorry she left—I didn't mean to upset her," Carole said stiffly. "But I don't understand what the big deal was. She's always getting upset. She's always running off. She was saying what a great night it was to go to Lover's Point, and she was talking about taking Kismet out there tonight. I told her I thought that would be a really stupid thing to do."

Louise looked horrified. Carole was pleased to see that her cousin at least seemed to agree with her point of view. "You mean she's going to the lake without me?" Louise said. "But she promised I could come. She said that she wouldn't go without me."

"I'm sure even Aunt Jessie isn't crazy enough to go tonight," Carole said. In her mind she heard Aunt Jessie say, "Don't you think I'm crazy?" Did she think her aunt was crazy? One thing was for sure. Aunt Jessie got upset so easily. But was she really crazy? Had Jackson Foley been crazy?

Carole stared at Louise. "Maybe you can talk some sense into Jessie. She went into the kitchen."

Louise ran out of the room. Carole shook her head as she watched her go. She was sick of both of them. Let them go off and sulk together!

Carole went off in search of sanity—hopefully in the person of Christina. But Christina was on the dance floor with Emile, smiling and happy, and Carole didn't want to bother her. She didn't feel like dancing just now. Instead she found Grand Alice, who was sitting in an easy chair tapping her feet to the music.

"You look flushed, child," Grand Alice said, catching

Carole's hand. "People keep rushing about. Sit down. Tell me, what's going on? Why are people upset at a party?"

Carole was beginning to feel pretty upset herself. "I don't know what's going on," she said. "Jessie said she was going to ride out to Lover's Point and I told her she shouldn't. I told her she might have screwed things up in her life before, but she shouldn't do it again—she shouldn't endanger Kismet like that. Jessie ran off and now Louise is mad and went off to be with Jessie. I don't know what's wrong with either of them."

Grand Alice looked very grave. "Oh, dear," she said slowly. "Oh, dear, you shouldn't have said that." She looked very unhappy.

"Said what?" Carole asked. She had a sudden feeling that she'd done something very wrong.

"Said that to Jessie. The very wrong thing to say," Grand Alice said. "You didn't know. How could you? But oh, dear, you shouldn't have."

"What is it?" she asked. "What did I say?"

"Let's go find a quiet place to talk," Grand Alice said grimly. She got up from her chair. "You'll need to hear the whole story now."

She led Carole into a small side room and closed the door. She sat down, and Carole sat down to listen.

"Fifteen years ago," Grand Alice began, "when Jessie was barely out of high school, she met a man named Lawrence Freeman. He was an artist. He liked her photographs. She liked his paintings. He was tall and funny and as much in love with her as she was in love with him. I never saw anyone love someone so much as Jessie loved Lawrence Freeman.

"They got married and moved to New York City. He painted and taught art at Hunter College, and Jessie took photographs full-time. They did well—they had a few art exhibitions and started selling some of their work, and they really enjoyed living in the city. They were as happy as they could be—even more so when, after two years, Jessie had a baby girl. They named their daughter Joy."

"That was the man and child in the photograph," Carole said.

Grand Alice nodded. "That's right."

If they were so happy, Carole thought, then why would Jessie leave? Why would she come back to Minnesota? She wanted to ask Grand Alice, but she made herself sit still and listen.

Grand Alice continued, "One fall weekend, they decided to take a short vacation. They rented a car and drove to the Berkshire hills in western Massachusetts to look at the fall foliage. The hills in New England are beautiful that time of year. They were driving down Route Nine, near Holyoke, when something went wrong. To this day we're not sure exactly what happened. Maybe something was spilled on the highway. Maybe something was wrong with the car. Anyhow, it skidded without warning, flipped over the guard rail, and tumbled down the embankment. Jessie was hardly hurt at all."

Carole shut her eyes. She was suddenly afraid that she knew what Grand Alice was going to say next.

"Lawrence and Joy were killed."

Grand Alice paused as if to compose herself. Carole didn't know what to say. Poor Aunt Jessie! She felt terrible, both for her aunt and about herself. Here she'd thought that Jessie had abandoned her family, and instead they'd been tragically killed. Carole knew that she

90

shouldn't make assumptions about other people. From now on, she promised herself, she would remember not to.

She reached out and held Grand Alice's hand. Grand Alice gave her a sad smile.

"Unfortunately, Jessie had been driving," Grand Alice went on. "No one blamed her for what happened—there were witnesses who saw the accident, and said that the car went completely out of control—but Jessie blamed herself. She still can't forgive herself. Now it seems like the only time she's ever happy is when she's taking photographs. It's the only time that she can completely forget about her family." Grand Alice shook her head. "We never talk about Lawrence and Joy, or New York, because it's easier for Jessie not to remember them."

Carole frowned. "But that doesn't make sense," she argued. "I don't understand that kind of attitude. My mom died—"

"I know, dear. I loved your momma. I don't forget her."

"But that's exactly what I mean," Carole insisted. "I would never want to forget her. In fact, my dad and I talk about her all the time. We talk about the things we used to do together, and we talk about what Mom would think or say if she were still alive. If she knew I had a horse, for instance. I need to talk about her. I never want to forget a single thing about her."

Grand Alice laid her hand against Carole's cheek, and Carole leaned against it for a moment. "You must understand that everyone grieves differently," she said gently. "Do you remember your mother's funeral—how some people were crying, and some were not?"

"Yes." Carole did remember.

"And you and your father, you weren't always sad the same amount at the same times, were you?" Carole shook her head. "People all mourn differently, Carole. They all deal with pain in different ways. Personally, I like your way better than Jessie's. I've lost a lot of loved ones in my life, and if I tried to forget them all I wouldn't have much memory left. But your case is different from Jessie's—you don't blame yourself for your mother's death. You don't feel guilty. And even if the circumstances were the same—well, people are different, that's all. You need to respect Jessie's right to forget just as she needs to respect your right to remember."

Carole thought that she understood. "I'll try," she said. "I guess I still don't really understand Jessie, but maybe I don't have to. I guess I shouldn't have said what I did, either. I think I'd better apologize."

"I think that's a good idea," Grand Alice said with a nod of her head. "You're a compassionate person, Carole. Be kind to Jessie. Her life has not been easy."

"Miss Alice?" Colonel Hanson knocked, then opened the door. "I came to see if you would favor me with a dance." He looked from Carole to Grand Alice and back again. "Or am I interrupting?"

"Carole and I just came in here for a quiet chat," Grand Alice said. "I think we're finished now."

"We were talking about Aunt Jessie," Carole said. "Grand Alice told me about Lawrence and Joy."

Colonel Hanson nodded slowly. "So now you know," he said. "Lawrence was a good man, Carole, and you would have liked him as an uncle. You and Joy might have been good friends." He sighed and ran his fingers through his hair. "I didn't like not telling you about them, Carole, but Jessie keeps that part of her life so private. . . . I thought you ought to hear it from this side of the family."

Carole nodded. After what Grand Alice had told her, she understood why her father had kept the secret.

"She knows now," Grand Alice said. "She's old enough to understand. And I'd be pleased to dance with you, grandson, only none of that fast stuff, do you hear me? When you get to my age, you move slow." She lifted her chin regally and held her hand up to Colonel Hanson with the grace of a queen. He laughed and helped her to her feet.

"A fox trot is all," he promised, leading her to the dance floor.

Carole leaned against the door frame and watched them. Christina's father's "lousy jazz" was back on the stereo, and her father and Grand Alice moved gently to its slow, soft beat.

She thought again about the story Grand Alice had told

her. She'd been so caught up in the idea of family history and bloodlines that she'd been overly ready—even eager— to believe that Jessie had behaved like Jackson Foley. That hadn't been the case at all. Jessie's anger and grief were nothing like Jackson's abandonment and betrayal. Clearly, Jessie was not much like Jackson. Maybe bloodlines weren't as important in humans as they were in horses.

Carole thought back—if Jessie had married Lawrence fifteen years ago, then Joy, if she had lived, would have been close to Carole's age. She would have been close to Louise's age too.

Suddenly Carole felt she had found a key to understanding the close, protective relationship between Jessie and Louise. Once when Carole had gone on rounds with Judy Barker, Pine Hollow's veterinarian, she had seen a mare whose foal had died at birth. The mare seemed lost and unhappy without a foal to care for, but over the next several weeks she had gradually "adopted" another foal, as a way to soothe her grief. She had licked and fussed over and even nursed her adoptive baby, and the foal, cared for by two attentive mothers, had thrived.

Jessie and Louise reminded Carole of that mare and foal. Who was Carole to say that they hadn't both benefited by being so close to each other? For a brief moment Carole envied Louise. If Jessie had been nearby when Carole's mother had died, perhaps they could have leaned on each other. Carole would have liked that.

The music ended, and the silence broke Carole out of her reverie. Her father and Grand Alice stopped dancing and Grand Alice took a seat at the edge of the dance floor. Colonel Hanson went into the kitchen and came back with something to drink for both of them. That was a good idea—Carole was thirsty too. Plus, Jessie and Louise had gone into the kitchen. Carole would get a soda and apologize to Jessie at the same time.

But the big room was empty except for two little kids racing toy cars across the tiled floor. Carole looked back into the party rooms, but she didn't see Jessie or Louise—or Christina either—there. She did see Emile, sitting by himself on the sofa. He waved to her, and she was just about to go ask him where everyone was when Christina came through the lean-to door.

A blast of icy air came in with her. Christina was heavily dressed in a thick parka and boots, with a scarf wrapped around and around her face. "Brrr! It's *really* getting cold out there!" she said to Carole through folds of scarf.

Carole helped her unwrap.

Christina's cold fingers fumbled with her parka zipper. "I'm half numb." She took off her hat and shook out her hair.

"Have you seen Louise?" Carole asked.

"Sure. That's where I've been. I just gave her a ride home on my snowmobile." Christina set her dripping snow boots on the mat by the door and hung up her coat on a hook. "She said she wasn't feeling well, but her parents are having fun and she didn't want to make them leave the party."

That didn't sound right to Carole. Louise had been feeling fine all day long. But why would she lie to Christina? Carole had a sudden bad feeling. "What about my aunt Jessie?" she asked. "Have you seen her?"

"Uh-uh." Christina shook her head. "I think she's gone, too, because her truck isn't in the driveway. Didn't she come over separately from the rest of you?"

"Yes." So Jessie was gone, and now Louise too. Carole still didn't believe that Jessie would ride out to Lover's Point, but clearly she had at least gone home. Gone home to sulk, Carole thought. No, that wasn't right—gone home because Carole had upset her. Carole felt like she had spoiled the party for both Jessie and Louise. In the back of her mind, she considered how disastrous it might be if Jessie actually did go to Lover's Point—but the front of her mind wouldn't let that be a possibility. Still, she felt responsible. She should do something. She would go home and persuade them both to come back to the party.

"Can I borrow your snowmobile?" she asked Christina. "I'd like to go home and check on Louise."

Christina frowned. "Gee, Carole, do you think that's really necessary? It's awfully cold out there, and I don't think Louise is very sick. She said she just had a bad headache. Stay here—you'll have fun with me and Emile."

"I know I would, but I'd rather be sure Louise is okay," Carole said. "I don't want to bother Aunt Lily and Uncle John either—Louise was right, they are having fun. But I'd really like to go." Carole smiled; she hoped persuasively. She didn't want to let Christina know how worried she felt.

Christina looked out the window and shivered. "It's just that I don't think I should let you go alone." She looked at Carole doubtfully.

"Oh, come on," said Carole. "There's no reason for you to get cold all over again. I'll wrap up and be careful, and besides, you know I can drive your snowmobile. It's not like I have to drive it on roads or anything—it's a straight shot home through the woods. I can follow the tracks you just made. They'll be easy to see in the bright moonlight."

"Well . . ." Christina looked into the living room. Emile waved and beckoned to her.

"Please," Carole said. "I'll come right back. You've already spent plenty of time away from Emile. I'll be careful, I promise."

"Okay. But do be careful." Christina handed Carole the snowmobile keys, and Carole ran upstairs to get her coat. She put it on quickly. She hoped everything would be all right.

11

THE WOODS FELT dangerous at night. The trees cast dark and terrible shadows under the full moon's bright light, and the heavy blanket of snow made stumps and fallen trees look menacingly large.

Carole, following the trail Christina had made, found herself becoming more and more frightened. She told herself firmly not to be scared. She reminded herself of how beautiful the trees were by daylight—how peaceful, how serene. She told herself that she had been in forests before: she had camped out many times; she had even ridden down a mountain trail in the dark. But then something swooped past her with a terrible screech and she felt panic rising in her throat. She tried not to scream.

She hit the throttle hard and the snowmobile shot

ahead. It was difficult to control on the uneven ground; it shook and rocked as it hit things she couldn't see. She was afraid to go too fast because she might hit something and wreck the snowmobile, but she was afraid to go too slowly because she wanted to get out of the woods as fast as she could.

She began to have a hard time following Christina's tracks—she couldn't see them very clearly—and looking up, she saw a huge bank of clouds sweeping in from the northwest to cover the bright moon. The clouds were moving fast. The wind was blowing hard, and Carole had never been so cold. Her stomach muscles tightened into a ball. Her teeth were clenched too hard to chatter. Already her fingers and feet were growing numb.

The woods grew darker. *Whump!* The snowmobile hit a fallen tree, careened off the top, and nearly overturned. Carole fought for her balance. It was worse than being on a bucking horse. At least a horse had some sense. The snowmobile did not. She gathered her courage around her and kept going.

The compound couldn't be too much farther ahead. She felt as if she'd been traveling for hours. She pushed the snowmobile as fast as she dared, faster and faster as the woods began to thin, and finally she saw lights ahead. A wave of relief washed over her.

The snowmobile began to slow down. Carole pushed the throttle harder, but the snowmobile sputtered and choked to a stop. Carole felt another flash of panic—had she broken it?—before she saw that the needle of the gas gauge pointed firmly to *E*. Empty. Out of gas.

Reluctantly she left the snowmobile in a snowdrift and struggled the rest of the way to the house on foot. A snowflake fell, and then another. She put up a mittened hand to catch them. Snow. This was what the dark clouds meant. There was going to be a storm.

Inside, the warm air greeted her like a friend. Ginger, Louise's dog, rushed up to her and began to lick her excitedly. "Down, Ginger," she murmured automatically. She quickly took off her sopping wet shoes, and shook the snow from her pant legs. "Hello?" she shouted. "Louise? Aunt Jessie?" No one answered. Carole ran through the house, calling their names. No one was there.

Next she tried Jessie's apartment. The lights were off and the rooms were dark and quiet. Then she tried the photo lab. The lights were on there, but the lab was empty. "They didn't really go, did they?" she asked Ginger, who was following her from room to room. Ginger wagged his tail. Carole felt almost sick. She looked around at Jessie's camera equipment, but the lab was too disorderly and Jessie had too many cameras for Carole to tell if anything was gone.

"We'll check the barn," she said to Ginger. At the door she pulled on the boots she had borrowed the day before and hurried back into the cold. Snow was falling, lightly but steadily.

The aisle light was burning brightly and the horses looked at her inquiringly. One horse, two—Carole counted them and her heart sank. Jiminy and Kismet were gone. Kismet's blanket was neatly folded and her stall door was latched shut, but Jiminy's door hung open and his blanket had been quickly tossed on the ground.

So, Carole thought, Jessie had gone out alone, and Louise had followed her in a hurry. Mechanically she picked up Jiminy's blanket. It was still warm from the heat of his body. Louise hadn't been gone long.

They must have gone to Lover's Point. It occurred to Carole that Aunt Jessie's recklessness might to some extent be because she really didn't care what happened to herself. That was okay for Aunt Jessie, maybe—but now her attitude involved not just herself, but Louise, Jiminy, and Kismet too. Something had to be done to stop them before one of them got hurt. Carole knew she was the only one who could do it.

She went back to the house to call for help, dripping snow across the kitchen floor. Frantically she searched the drawers for the phone book. What was Christina's last name? She thought hard. Johnson! She had to take off her mittens to open the phone book—and then she stared at the page in dismay. Of the hundred or so families listed in the tiny directory, eighteen were named Johnson. She looked in the drawer where she'd found the phone book, then back at the phone. It had a row of autodial buttons—one was labeled "Christina." She pushed it thankfully, and put the receiver to her ear.

Nothing. Not even a dial tone. She whacked the *reset* button over and over, and jiggled the cord in its socket, but nothing happened. The phone was dead. Carole remembered Aunt Jessie's words: *"The roads aren't always passable, and the phones don't always work."* She couldn't call Christina's house. She couldn't use the snowmobile either.

She thought of the other two horses. They weren't as fast as the snowmobile, but they were the only alternative she had. She didn't have time to waste. She would saddle up Spice and go after them herself.

She went back to the barn and rummaged through the tack trunk. What would she need in an emergency? She found some rope, and a few extra stirrup leathers that she thought might be useful. She slung all of them over her shoulder. In the bottom of the trunk she found a large gray flashlight, and she took that as well.

Next she led Spice to the aisle where she could saddle him. The big horse stood quietly, blinking as if half asleep. Carole's hands shook as she tightened the wide girth and buckled the bridle. She grabbed the flashlight and reins together in her left hand, and hauled herself up onto Spice's broad back.

Never mount inside the barn, she heard Max's voice inside

her head. *If the horse should rear up under the doorway, you'd be in trouble.*

She turned Spice's head toward the woods. Max's voice, once begun, wouldn't stop reminding her of all the safety rules she was about to violate. Never go out alone, in unfamiliar territory. Be very careful riding at night. You can't see danger spots, and neither can your horse. Never go out in bad weather. You'll increase your odds of having an accident, and increase the odds that the accident will cause injury.

Carole was doing everything wrong. I do know better, she said to herself, but I haven't got any other choice. Right now she was more worried about Louise and Jessie than she was about herself. She couldn't shake the feeling that something was very wrong, that her aunt and cousin were already somehow in trouble.

Willing though Spice was, Carole wished she were riding Jiminy, the sturdy Morgan, or Kismet, the stalwart Arabian. She hoped Spice had the courage, ability, and steadiness to do what she needed him to do. Still he was the best horse she had. She had no choice but to take him.

She shouted to Ginger and gave Spice a cluck and a kick to send him forward. They rode out into the darkness. Ginger followed. The wind blew stiff and cold, and the snow was falling hard.

CAROLE RODE WITH the reins in one hand. With the other she held the flashlight up like a beacon or headlight in front of her. The thin beam of light shone faintly in the dark woods. It illuminated a line straight in front of her, but seemed to throw the sides of the trail into deeper shadow. The woods were no less scary than they had been before—and this time the roar of the snowmobile's engine wasn't there to mask the eerie silence. Carole was not used to a world whose sounds were muffled by snow. The wind blew and sometimes whispered through the pine trees, but there was no other noise except Spice's breathing and the beating of her own heart.

She squinted into the falling snow. The flakes burned her cheeks and the wind made her eyes water so that she could hardly see. She tried desperately to be sure where she was going. What if she couldn't remember the way? The trees looked so different in the dark. She had to find the lake. Otherwise she would be lost. She could freeze to death quickly in the cold.

Spice was a comfort. At least she knew she wasn't alone, and she felt a little less scared on horseback. Spice couldn't find the lake for her, but he could and was carrying her safely through the storm. She wondered if he sensed how much her life depended on him. She hoped he wouldn't let her down.

"Ginger!" she called. The dog had kept close to Spice's heels at the start, but now he was gone. She turned around in the saddle to look, but couldn't see or hear him any-where. She hoped he was okay. Had he been hurt? She tried not to worry about him. She had too many other things to worry about now.

She was so cold that she could barely move. Her legs felt like lead; she almost couldn't feel her feet. The flashlight wavered and she nearly dropped it; instead, she tucked it under her arm and clamped her elbow firmly to her side. She switched the reins from hand to hand and tried to warm the other hand in the pocket of her parka.

She yawned. The cold was making her sleepy. Suddenly she sat up straight, alarmed. The cold would make her sleepy, but if she lost her ability to concentrate she'd get lost and freeze for sure. She had to think of something to keep her mind busy.

She thought of Jessie, Lawrence, and Joy. She thought about the story of Jackson Foley, and the story of the unknown woman from Africa, who had come across the ocean with the amulet Carole was now wearing around her neck. She had endured much more danger and suffering than Carole was facing right now. How had the woman survived all of it—the slave boat, the auction, the horrible harshness of her life? She wondered how many daughters the woman had had, and how the daughter who next wore the amulet had felt about it.

Her family was all of those people. It reached across thousands of miles and hundreds of years. So many of them she didn't know and would never know—some had been lost forever. Some of them had been good people, and some of them had not been so good. But who was she to judge? They were just people, after all, doing their best—sometimes right, sometimes wrong.

Her head nodded despite herself and she yawned again. She couldn't let herself be tired. She forced her back straight and took a firmer grip on the reins, which helped her stay on when Spice suddenly stumbled. Carole pitched forward onto his shoulder, then back into the saddle when he righted himself. It shook her up, and shook her awake.

She looked around closely. The terrain was rougher, as it should be—they were getting close to the lake. And Spice was making his way through the heavy going and uneven footing with diligence and surety. His head was lowered, but his steps were steady. The wind blew harder, and made a funny muffled sound.

"Good boy, Spice," she said, leaning low on his neck. "Good boy, it's not much farther. Come on." Catching her urgency, he plunged forward. The muffled sound came again and Spice's ears shot to attention. He brought himself to a quivering halt and whinnied loud and high. For a moment Carole thought the sound would shatter the frozen forest. She leaned forward in her stirrups to see what was wrong.

Something was moving in the woods ahead—something large, something fast. In her flashlight's beam she caught a glimpse of white. Then she recognized the sound—it was the gallop of a fleeing horse, made awkward and muffled by the deep snow.

Kismet raced past them, his saddle empty and the stirrups flying. Spice shrieked again, and whirled to follow Kismet, but he obeyed Carole when she forced him to turn back around and go the way Kismet had come.

Carole's mouth was dry. She knew then that she had been right to follow Jessie and Louise. Someone was going to need her help.

Spice gave another little cry. This time Carole recognized the figure of a horse right away—a horse and rider. Jiminy Cricket and Louise. "Louise!" she shouted.

107

The figure waved frantically. "Carole! Carole, hurry!"
Carole raced to her side. "It's Jessie . . . Kismet . . ."
Louise had been crying. She was clearly terrified—her body
shook with fear and cold.

"I just saw Kismet," Carole said, speaking calmly in order to sooth Louise.

"Jessie . . ." Louise gulped down another sob.

"Where is Jessie?"

"On the ice—stuck in rocks. Oh, Carole, I don't know
what to do!"

Carole pushed Spice closer to Jiminy and reached out to
touch Louise's arm. "It'll be okay," she said, in the gentle
voice she'd used when little May Grover fell off her pony.
"It'll be fine. Tell me what happened, so we can go help
Jessie."

Louise nodded tearfully. "She was up on the rocks. She
wanted to get a picture from a certain angle, and she
couldn't quite get it. She kept asking Kismet to turn—and
she wasn't paying attention to the footing. Kismet slipped
on the ice and threw her. She's fallen into a crevice in the
rocks, and she's hurt and she can't get out." Louise drew in
a quivering breath. "I've got to get help—I've got to get
home—but it's going to take too long and I don't know
what to do."

Her last words were an anguished cry. Carole understood
and agreed. It was too cold for Jessie to lie unmoving. She

would freeze to death before either Carole or Louise could get back to her with help.

"We'll have to save her ourselves," Carole said.

"But I don't know what to do," Louise wailed. Carole felt a moment's frustration. By getting so upset, Louise was only making things worse. Carole wished fervently that Stevie and Lisa were there to help her. Together the three of them could do anything—and right now, she needed Stevie's ingenuity and Lisa's logic as well as her own horse sense.

Good friends never leave you, she told herself. They're always with you. The thought gave her the courage to go on.

"Show me where Jessie is," she commanded Louise. Louise nodded and turned Jiminy around, and Carole urged Spice after them.

At the edge of the lake Lover's Point looked like a rocky finger pointing to the sky. Louise pulled Jiminy to a halt and gestured to a spot halfway up the slope. Carole nodded. She could see Jessie, a dark shape against the snow-covered rocks. "Stay here until I need you," she told Louise, and she cautiously walked Spice onto the rocks.

Carole paid attention to the footing. She watched for sharp juts of rock and bits of glare ice and tried to steer Spice around them, but otherwise she gave him his head. He climbed the slope with the agility of a mountain pony. When they were near Aunt Jessie, Carole stopped him and dismounted. "Stand," she said gently, laying her hand against his chest. Spice lowered his ears and stood patiently. Carole began to think that she would trust him to do anything.

She knelt in the snow. "Aunt Jessie, Aunt Jessie," she called. Her aunt didn't move or open her eyes.

"Go 'way," Jessie mumbled. Carole had to lean in to hear her words above the wind.

"Where are you hurt?" Carole shouted. She was afraid to move Jessie without first finding out what was wrong. Jessie might have hurt her back or her head—Carole knew she could make things worse by moving her.

"I don't know; she isn't home right now," said Jessie.

"Where are you hurt?" Carole shouted again.

There was a pause. Jessie opened her eyes and seemed to be considering the question. "The light meter isn't set right," she said finally.

Carole felt desperate. Jessie wasn't making any sense—was she just too tired? Was she falling asleep from the cold? "Are you falling asleep?" Carole bellowed.

Jessie smiled. "Yes, ma'am. Nice sleep. Good night." She shut her eyes again.

Carole had to wake her up. What could she do to make Jessie respond to her? What would Stevie do in a situation like this?

Suddenly she bent her face to Jessie's ear. "Knock, knock," she said loudly.

Jessie's eyelids flickered open. "What?"

"Knock, knock," Carole repeated.

"Who's there?" Jessie responded automatically.

"Banana."

"Banana who?"

"Knock, knock."

"Who's there?"

"Banana."

"Banana who?" This time Jessie definitely looked more alert.

"Knock, knock," Carole said. One good thing about this joke was that it was long.

"Who's there?" Now Jessie looked irritated.

"Orange," Carole said.

Jessie smiled. "Orange who?"

"Orange you glad I didn't say banana?"

Jessie laughed. "No more bananas." She blinked, and said in a tone of recognition, "Carole."

"That's right, it's me," Carole said. "We're going to get you home. But first tell me where you're hurt."

"My arm. My left arm."

"Anywhere else?"

"No." Jessie grimaced. "Believe me, that's enough. It's hurt so badly that I can't pull myself out."

"Top of your arm or bottom?"

"Bottom. Below my elbow."

"Okay." Carole examined the way Jessie lay. Her hips

had been caught between a gap in the rocks. Her left arm had come down hard on a rock, but her head and shoulders were not trapped. "If I hold you up, can you wiggle free?"

They tried it. Jessie gasped when her arm moved. She began to shiver uncontrollably.

"How are you stuck?" Carole asked.

"It's more of an . . . in-and-out . . . than an up-and-down," Jessie said between clenched teeth.

Carole rocked back on her heels to study the problem. What would Lisa do? Carole decided to try the only approach that came to her. She took the rope she had brought and passed it under Jessie's arms and across her back. With one of the stirrup leathers she tied Jessie's upper left arm tight against her side to keep her forearm from moving. She tied the loop of rope against Jessie's body. With the long ends she made another loop and put that over the horn on Spice's Western saddle. She went back to Jessie's side. "Pull, Spice!" she ordered.

Spice began to strain against the rope. Jessie slowly slid free, crying out in pain. Carole tried to ease her down into the snow. "Whoa!" she shouted. Spice stopped, and Carole untied the makeshift harness.

Jessie was so cold that she had a hard time standing, even with Carole to support her. Carole felt that she could hardly move herself. The snow was thickening and she could barely see Louise, who stood anxiously on the edge of the lake.

"She's okay!" Carole tried to shout, but now her voice seemed lost. Her lips were numb. She raised her arm in a half wave instead, and Louise waved back.

She maneuvered Jessie to Spice's side, and held her against the horse's thick fur, hoping that Jessie could feel some of the warmth of Spice's body. Jessie moaned and tried to support her left arm with her right. Carole undid the leather that tied Jessie's upper arm down and used it and the other leather to make a sort of sling.

"Is that better?" she whispered. She could feel her own movements becoming uncertain and weak.

"Thank you," Jessie whispered. She closed her eyes and leaned against Spice's shoulder. To Carole the horse suddenly seemed to have grown to twice his normal size. He was so big. How were they going to get Jessie into the saddle?

Carole usually mounted a horse so automatically that she didn't think about what she was doing. Left foot in the left stirrup, left hand grabs the pommel, right leg swings over—but Jessie couldn't use her left hand. Could she mount from the right? Riders never did—it would seem awkward. But she said to Jessie, "Let's turn you around." She put her hands gently on Jessie's shoulders.

A gust of wind hit them so hard that Carole fell to her knees against Spice. Jessie cried out. Carole wanted to sob. She'd tried so hard, but she was so cold. What if she couldn't get them home?

113

"Come on," she said to herself and to Jessie, and she used Spice's leg to haul herself back to her feet.

She heard a faint sharp noise like a dog barking and the wind became a roar. On the bank Louise shouted. Carole saw a light bouncing through the woods. A pair of lights— headlights! It was a snowmobile, flying at top speed!

Ginger rushed out of the woods and flung himself at Jiminy's legs, barking madly. The snowmobile, with two people on board, came partway up the rocky point and slid to a stop in front of Carole and Jessie. Uncle John cut the engine and climbed off, but Carole's father was already by her side. He looked down at her and Carole felt tears of relief come to her eyes.

"Jessie's hurt," she said. Colonel Hanson went to Jessie and gently helped lower her to the snowmobile seat. Uncle John wrapped a thick blanket around Carole's shoulders. "How did you know to come?" Carole asked him.

Uncle John grinned with a mixture of joy and relief. "That mutt," he said, pointing to Ginger, who now came cavorting up to Carole. "He came all the way to Christina's house and stood outside whining and barking. When we saw him, we figured something was wrong. Christina said that you had all gone home. Once we got there, we followed your tracks—Spice leaves a big trail, and the wind hadn't blown it shut yet." He bent over Carole and gave her a warm hug. "Let's go home," he said.

Carole thought that was the best idea she'd ever heard.

CAROLE WOKE UP when she heard a car door slam. Bright sunlight was streaming in through the open curtains of the guest room windows.

Carole jumped up, then looked down at herself and laughed. She was still wearing the sweater and jeans she had worn to the party last night. She had been so tired from her adventure that right now she could hardly remember walking into the bedroom, much less climbing into bed. She did remember seeing Spice safely into his stall—and Kismet, too, who had come home on her own— with lots of hay and an extra helping of oats. She also recalled watching Uncle John bundle Jessie into the truck to take her to the hospital, and sitting, sleepy-eyed, at the kitchen table with Louise while Aunt Lily made them hot chocolate and fussed over them. After that, nothing. She had slept a long time.

Carole looked out the window. Uncle John had come back from the hospital, and he had brought Aunt Jessie back with him. Carole watched him walk around the front of the truck, open the passenger door, and gently help Jessie out. Jessie had a large white cast from her fingertips to just past her elbow, but otherwise she looked fine. Carole felt a rush of relief. She flew down the hall to greet them.

Aunt Lily opened the door. "Well, well," she said softly. "Jessie, you look a sight better this morning than you did last night."

"That's right," Jessie said with a small smile as she walked in the door. "I feel a sight better too."

Carole stopped before she had quite reached them. She wasn't sure what to say to Jessie. Jessie turned and saw Carole, and her smile faded. "Good morning, Carole," she said. Her voice was deep and serious.

"Good morning," Carole said.

"I have a lot I want to say to you. Can we talk now? It's important."

"Sure." Carole followed Jessie into the living room and sat down on the sofa beside her. She felt a little unsure of herself. This Jessie—this serious, quiet Jessie—was unlike the Jessie she was used to.

"I owe you a big apology, and a big thank-you too,"

Jessie began. "I'm very embarrassed by what happened last night."

"Anyone can fall off a horse," said Carole politely. "I've done it myself lots—"

"That's not what I mean, and you know it," Jessie said, with a hint of her usual sharpness. "Carole, if all I had done last night was fall off Kismet, I wouldn't be sorry. But I fell off because I had ridden my horse onto ice and rocks at night—I fell off because I made my horse take me somewhere that was dangerous for both me and her. I did something foolish and reckless—and what's worse, I endangered you and Louise too.

"You have to believe me when I say that it never occurred to me that Louise would try to follow me, or that you would either. I definitely did not mean to involve the two of you. But I'm old enough now that I should have known better—and I'm very, very sorry."

"It's okay," Carole said. "I never thought you meant to hurt anyone."

"If I recall, you said that you didn't think I was thinking at all," Jessie said with a grin. She shifted her heavy cast so that the weight of it rested on her knee.

"Oh, that . . ." Carole blushed, recalling their argument at the party. "I should never have said what I said."

"No, no, you were at least correct," Jessie said. "If I recall, I was a whole lot ruder to you, and with less reason.

I tend to fly off the handle about some things, and I'm sorry about that too. And if I implied that you were a Southern softie—well, that was a total lie. You're a very capable person, Carole, and it's lucky for me that you are. You're an excellent horsewoman too." Aunt Jessie laughed. "Anyone tells you different, send 'em to me and I'll lick 'em for you. I promise. After last night, I owe you one."

"I'm just glad you aren't badly hurt," Carole said. Remembering how terrified she had been last night, she couldn't feel that a broken arm was much to worry about.

Aunt Jessie seemed to agree. "This is nothing," she said, gesturing to her cast. "It's even on my left arm, so I can still take pictures. I've got bruises you wouldn't believe, but on the whole I'm remarkably sound. Not even frostbitten. How about you?"

"Tired," Carole said. "Just tired, and . . . glad it's over, I guess."

"Me too," Jessie said. "But Carole, tell me one thing. I seem to remember hearing some horrible knock-knock joke in the middle of the storm last night. Was that you?"

"No, that was Stevie," Carole said, with a straight face and an inward laugh. Aunt Jessie looked puzzled, but Carole didn't explain. She didn't mind if Jessie thought she had some mystery about her too. "But Aunt Jessie," she continued, "I first went looking for you last night because I wanted to apologize. I'm sorry I went snooping into your life where I didn't belong. I didn't mean to hurt you—I didn't know that I would. I'm just learning to respect that people have to do things their own way."

Jessie leaned against the back of the sofa. "Your way is a good way too," she said. "I admire you for having the strength to remember what you've lost. Maybe someday I'll be able to think the way you do."

A sudden tear came to Jessie's eye. "Oh, Carole, I miss your momma so much," she whispered. "You remind me so much of her—she was my big sister, and I always looked up to her. I know she'd be proud of what a lovely and courageous young woman you've become." She reached out to hug Carole, and Carole felt herself held tight against Jessie's chest. It was a good feeling. "I have so many stories to tell you about your mother," Jessie said.

Carole sat up and wiped her eyes where a few quick tears had started to form. "I'd like that," she said. "I'd really like that. Anytime you want to talk, I want to listen."

Jessie smiled, and this time Carole could see in her smile a combination of the brash, sometimes rude aunt she had first met and the thoughtful, solemn one who had just come home from the hospital. Different sides of the same person, she thought to herself. She hadn't realized how wonderfully complex people—and life—could be.

"I'll talk to you soon," Jessie promised. "I'll start today, and I'll call you down in Virginia whenever I think of something good. But right now, Niece, I need a nap. They don't let you sleep much in the emergency room." With another smile, she got up and walked stiffly down the hall.

Carole found her father, Aunt Lily, and Louise in the kitchen talking to Uncle John. Aunt Lily had started to fry a pan of sausages and potatoes for Uncle John, and when she saw Carole she added more food to the pan. Carole was content to eat breakfast and listen to them talk. She felt too content—and too tired—to speak.

Louise got up from the table. "Um . . . Carole? I was going to go to the photo lab—I got a camera for Christmas and Jessie's teaching me to develop my own pictures. There's some work I wanted to do. Do you want to come? I could tell you all about it," she said. She gave Carole a tentative, but very real, smile.

Carole appreciated the offer. "I would," she said, "but I really wanted to go check on the horses. Spice was wonderful last night, and I'd like to thank him."

Louise understood. "I've already been out to feed them," she said, "but I know Spice would enjoy the attention. You're right—he deserves it!"

Carole waded through the hip-high snow to the barn, following the trail Louise had broken. Inside, the horses' breath made the air warm and humid and sunlight shone through the barred windows. The air smelled like horse. Carole breathed in deeply and happily. "Hello, everyone," she said. "Hello, Spice." She opened his stall and offered him a sugar lump. Her pockets were bulging with carrots and apples.

Spice perked his ears and lipped the sugar from her palm. Carole gave him a big hug, then settled herself on the huge pile of hay in the corner of his stall. "We need to talk," she said. Spice nodded his head—probably to ask for more sugar, but Carole chose to think he was agreeing with her. She gave him a carrot.

"Exactly. Because you were super last night. And I have to apologize," she said. "I didn't think that you were as good a horse as the Morgan or the Arabian. I was wrong." She gave him an apple, which he ate in dainty bites, his huge nose nestled in her hand. "Bloodlines can tell you some things about horses—I don't think you're as fast as Secretariat, no matter what—but they can't tell you about a horse's heart. Your heart, Spice, is pure champion Thoroughbred."

Spice looked at her calmly. He seemed to be waiting for her to continue. She gave him another carrot. Suddenly she remembered the birthday party Stevie and Lisa had planned for Prancer. New Year's Day was the Thoroughbreds' birthday, and this was New Year's Day!

"You've got a Thoroughbred's heart," she repeated. She gave Spice another apple, and while he ate it she sang "Happy Birthday" to him. It seemed appropriate.

121

After that she gave treats to the other three horses and sang "Happy Birthday" to them too. After all, Jiminy and Kismet had shared the ordeal, too, and each had done well. Carole knew better than to blame Kismet for slipping on the ice, or for being frightened when Jessie fell. And Sugar, she was sure, would have been just as willing to go out as Spice was. "I love you all," Carole assured them.

Back in the house Jessie had moved to the living room sofa with an afghan and a pillow. Louise was sitting on the sofa's end, showing Jessie the pictures she'd just finished developing. Carole knelt beside them to look. To her surprise, some of the pictures were of her—taken unawares as she hugged Uncle John in the airport and drove the snowmobile with Christina behind her.

"Some of these are very good," Aunt Jessie said approvingly. "I bet Carole would like to see more. Why don't you get some of the stuff from my files, Louise?" Louise ran to get them. "Would you like that?" Aunt Jessie demanded of Carole.

"Definitely," she answered. "I want to see all the interesting, confusing angles." Aunt Jessie grinned.

They were deeply engrossed in photographs when Colonel Hanson came in. "I don't want to bother you," he said. "I enjoy seeing the three of you together like this, and you look like you're having fun. But Carole, if you want Aunt Lily and me to wash any of your clothes before we go back, give them to me now. We'll have to pack tonight—we leave for home pretty early tomorrow."

Carole nodded, but a sudden thought made her pause.

"What is it?" her father asked.

"Just for a minute," she said, "this felt like it was home."

14

"HEY, STARLIGHT, DID you miss me?" Carole held up her hand. Starlight lowered his head and blew into it gently. To Carole, it seemed as if he were saying yes. It was early in the morning, the day after they'd flown back to Pine Hollow. Her dad had dropped her off at the stable on his way to work. She couldn't wait to see Starlight again. "I sure missed you," she told him.

"So did we," said Lisa, coming around the corner with Stevie close behind. "Miss *you*, I mean, not Starlight. We couldn't have missed him—we took good care of him for you."

"The best," Stevie confirmed. They hugged Carole, and she hugged them back.

"You're here early," Carole told them.

"We wanted to see you. We knew you'd get here early," Lisa said. "How was your trip?"

"I'm glad I went, and I had a great time, but it's good to be home," Carole said. "Tell me everything—what happened while I was gone?"

"Saddle Club meeting?" suggested Lisa.

"Of course!" They sat down on some hay bales in the aisle and Stevie passed around the last of her Christmas candy. There wasn't much—her brothers had gotten into it —but it was better than nothing.

"Not much happened with us," said Stevie, crunching a candy cane. "Except, of course, Karenna came to visit. I don't know about her, Carole. We liked her well enough, but we kept expecting her to be more like you. She was into malls, and makeup, and Meg and Betsy—all things that you're not into, and that we're not into. I never felt like we had much in common."

"We tried hard to be friends with her," Lisa said, "and I think she wanted to be our friend, but it never seemed to happen." Lisa shook her head and took another bite of peanut brittle.

"I understand," Carole assured them. She picked through the small bag of candy and found a piece of pink ribbon candy. "I'm glad you were here to make her feel welcome even if she wasn't exactly your cup of tea. I know what you mean about the mall and stuff, but I'm just kind

125

of used to her. We were good friends when we lived on the same base—there wasn't much to do there except ride.

"And just as you were there for me with Karenna, you were also there for me at Lover's Point," she said. Stevie and Lisa leaned forward, interested.

"Lover's Point?" asked Stevie. "Sounds like a romance novel. What did it look like? Maybe we should name some-place around here—"

"Tell us what happened," Lisa said.

Carole told them the whole story of Aunt Jessie's accident and rescue. "I tried to think of what the two of you would do," she said. She explained how she had used Stevie's joke to get Jessie's attention, and Lisa's logic to free her from the rocks.

"What joke did you tell her?" Stevie wanted to know.

"The banana knock-knock joke," Carole said. "You know, the one that goes on and on. It was the only knock-knock joke I could think of, and I wanted her to have to talk to me."

"Oh, you should have told her the other long one," Stevie said, with a disappointed shake of her head. "It's much better."

"The other one? I don't remember it."

"How could you not remember it?" asked Stevie. "It's only the greatest knock-knock joke of all time. Knock, knock," she said severely.

"Who's there?" Lisa and Carole asked obediently.

126

"Will you remember me tomorrow?"

"Will you remember me tomorrow who?"

Stevie frowned. "No, you're supposed to answer the question," she said. "Try it again. Knock, knock."

"Who's there?" they asked in chorus.

"Will you remember me in the morning?"

"Yes," they said.

"Knock, knock," repeated Stevie.

"Who's there?"

"I thought you said you'd remember me," Stevie said, rolling with laughter. Carole and Lisa giggled and groaned.

"How was the family-tree project?" asked Lisa. "Did you find any great and famous ancestors that you're destined to take after?" She leaned forward, her chin in her hand. She was partially joking, but she thought it would be nice if Carole did come from someone famous. Lisa's mother was interested in ancestry.

Carole shook her head. "No. I learned a lot of history, though, and a lot of good stories I don't want to forget."

"What was your family like?" Lisa asked. "My mom's always talking about our heritage and traditions, but she means I have to have good manners and act ladylike." Lisa grimaced. "She never tells me anything about people."

Carole thought about Jessie and Jackson, Grand Alice and her almost-forgotten sister Sophie. She thought about all the pictures that she'd seen. How could she explain it all to her two best friends?

"My family is just like most other families," she said at last. "Mostly full of people who tried to do what was right, only some of them did a better job than others. People are people, no matter what." She struggled for a way to make Stevie and Lisa understand. "I learned that who you're related to or descended from doesn't change who you are. The only thing that matters in your life is what you do and how you do it."

She pulled the wooden amulet out from where she'd tucked it into the top of her sweater. She wouldn't wear it every day, but she'd worn it today to show Lisa and Stevie. "My great-grandmother gave this to me," she said, stroking the little animal softly with her fingertip. "Her—I don't know, great-great, lots of greats—her ancestor wore it when she came to this country on a slave ship. It came from Africa."

"Wow!" Stevie and Lisa leaned close. "And she kept it safe," Stevie marveled. "It hardly even looks old."

"It must give you shivers to wear it," Lisa said, looking at Carole closely.

"It does," Carole admitted. "I feel so close to that woman, even though I'll never know anything about her except that she was a slave and that she gave this to her daughter. Her life must have been harder than anything I can imagine, but she saved this and passed it on to her family. It makes me feel like I can do anything with my life. It reminds me that anything's possible."

"It reminds you of how much you love horses," Stevie added softly. Carole nodded and tucked the amulet safely away.

"I'll let you look at it again later," she promised. "I've got a lot to show you. Grand Alice gave me one of her oil paintings—a really pretty one of Lover's Point in the summertime—and Jessie and Louise gave me a whole bunch of photographs. There's one of a row of icicles, and there's a whole bunch of pictures of the family, even some of me and my mom when I was a baby. And Louise gave me the picture of me and Christina on the snowmobile—"

"Wait a minute," Stevie cut in. "You rode a snowmobile?"

"I *drove* a snowmobile," Carole corrected her. "It was fun, but I'll take Starlight any day. He's easier to steer, and he never runs out of gas." They laughed. "That reminds me. I brought a bunch of treats for him, to make up for being gone so long."

"He deserves them too," Lisa said. "He never got his share of the birthday party, remember, Stevie? Because Karenna was riding him on the trails. We meant to give it to him later, but we forgot."

Carole was quick to ask what birthday party. Wasn't Prancer's party just for Thoroughbreds? "Starlight's not a Thoroughbred," she said.

"Oh, we decided that it wasn't fair to ignore the other horses," said Lisa. "We gave them all treats. Luckily,

Stevie'd brought enough carrots to feed all of Pine Hollow. We sang 'Happy Birthday' to them all too."

"You sang 'Happy Birthday' to every horse?" Carole asked.

"We couldn't think of a better plan," Stevie said apologetically. "My mind's been so preoccupied lately." She glanced significantly in the direction of No-Name's stall.

"But that's exactly what I did!" Carole told them how she'd sung to all four of the Foleys' horses on New Year's Day.

"Weird," said Stevie, shaking her head. "I mean, *weird*. The same idea, over one-thousand miles apart—"

"Not weird," Lisa corrected her firmly. "After all, we're all best friends and we all think alike. What could be more natural? Now, let's go give Starlight his share."

They sang to Starlight and petted him, but he seemed to like the apples better than their singing. "Ungrateful horse," Stevie said. "Now, my mare, on the other hand, loves to hear me sing—"

"Stevie's horse is perfect," Lisa said, teasing her.

"Yes," agreed Carole, "but does she have a name?" Stevie groaned and shook her head. They went down the aisle to visit No-Name.

"Still No-Name," Stevie said sadly. "I haven't had any brilliant ideas. I think the cold must be affecting my brain."

"If you think this is cold . . ." said Carole, remembering her night at Lover's Point. "Trust me, Stevie, you haven't been to Minnesota!"

Stevie played with No-Name's forelock and pretended not to hear. "I have progressed to the point of abandoning a completely Arabian name," she said. "Lisa was right. She's half American—half southern American at that. I don't want to ignore either side of her." She looked at Lisa mischievously. "Do you remember suggesting Scarlett O'Hara and Robert E. Lee?"

"Sure," said Lisa.

"Well, I've been thinking maybe a combination name would work. How about Muhammad O'Lee?"

Lisa leaned against the stall, shaking her head with laughter. Carole reached into her coat pocket and handed Stevie a pen.

"What's that for?" asked Stevie.

"For you," said Carole. "Back to the drawing board."

The rest of The Saddle Club agreed.

About the Author

BONNIE BRYANT is the author of more than sixty books for young readers, including novelizations of movie hits such as *Teenage Mutant Ninja Turtles*® and *Honey, I Blew Up the Kid*, written under her married name, B. B. Hiller.

Ms. Bryant began writing The Saddle Club in 1986. Although she had done some riding before that, she intensified her studies then and found herself learning right along with her characters Stevie, Carole, and Lisa. She claims that they are all much better riders than she is.

Ms. Bryant was born and raised in New York City. She lives in Greenwich Village with her two sons.

Saddle Up For Fun!

Join The Saddle Club

As an official Saddle Club member you'll get:

- *Saddle Club newsletter*
- *Saddle Club membership card*
- *Saddle Club bookmark*
- *and exciting updates on everything that's happening with your favorite series.*

Bantam Doubleday Dell Books for Young Readers
Saddle Club Membership Box BK
1540 Broadway
New York, NY 10036

SKYLARK

Bantam Doubleday Dell
Books for Young Readers

Name _____

Address _____

City _____ State _____ Zip _____

Date of birth _____

THE SADDLE CLUB™

❏ 15594-6 HORSE CRAZY #1	$3.50/$4.50 Can.	
❏ 15611-X HORSE SHY #2	$3.25/$3.99 Can.	
❏ 15626-8 HORSE SENSE #3	$3.50/$4.50 Can.	
❏ 15637-3 HORSE POWER #4	$3.50/$4.50 Can.	
❏ 15703-5 TRAIL MATES #5	$3.50/$4.50 Can.	
❏ 15728-0 DUDE RANCH #6	$3.50/$4.50 Can.	
❏ 15754-X HORSE PLAY #7	$3.25/$3.99 Can.	
❏ 15769-8 HORSE SHOW #8	$3.25/$3.99 Can.	
❏ 15780-9 HOOF BEAT #9	$3.50/$4.50 Can.	
❏ 15790-6 RIDING CAMP #10	$3.50/$4.50 Can.	
❏ 15805-8 HORSE WISE #11	$3.25/$3.99 Can..	
❏ 15821-X RODEO RIDER #12	$3.50/$4.50 Can.	
❏ 15832-5 STARLIGHT CHRISTMAS #13	$3.50/$4.50 Can.	
❏ 15847-3 SEA HORSE #14	$3.50/$4.50 Can.	
❏ 15862-7 TEAM PLAY #15	$3.50/$4.50 Can.	
❏ 15882-1 HORSE GAMES #16	$3.25/$3.99 Can.	
❏ 15937-2 HORSENAPPED #17	$3.50/$4.50 Can.	
❏ 15928-3 PACK TRIP #18	$3.50/$4.50 Can.	

❏ 15938-0 STAR RIDER #19	$3.50/$4.50 Can.	
❏ 15907-0 SNOW RIDE #20	$3.50/$4.50 Can.	
❏ 15983-6 RACEHORSE #21	$3.50/$4.50 Can.	
❏ 15990-9 FOX HUNT #22	$3.50/$4.50 Can.	
❏ 48025-1 HORSE TROUBLE #23	$3.50/$4.50 Can.	
❏ 48067-7 GHOST RIDER #24	$3.50/$4.50 Can.	
❏ 48072-3 SHOW HORSE #25	$3.50/$4.50 Can.	
❏ 48073-1 BEACH RIDE #26	$3.50/$4.50 Can.	
❏ 48074-X BRIDLE PATH #27	$3.50/$4.50 Can.	
❏ 48075-8 STABLE MANNERS #28	$3.50/$4.50 Can.	
❏ 48076-6 RANCH HANDS #29	$3.50/$4.50 Can.	
❏ 48077-4 AUTUMN TRAIL #30	$3.50/$4.50 Can.	
❏ 48145-2 HAYRIDE #31	$3.50/$4.50 Can.	
❏ 48146-0 CHOCOLATE HORSE #32	$3.50/$4.50 Can.	
❏ 48147-9 HIGH HORSE #33	$3.50/$4.50 Can.	
❏ 48148-7 HAY FEVER #34	$3.50/$4.50 Can.	
❏ 48149-5 A SUMMER WITHOUT HORSES Super #1	$3.99/$4.99 Can.	

Bantam Doubleday Dell
Books For Young Readers

Bantam Books, Dept. SC35,
2451 South Wolf Road, Des Plaines, IL 60018   DA60

Please send the items I have checked above. I am enclosing $_____ (please add $2.50 to cover postage and handling). Send check or money order, no cash or C.O.D.s please.

Mr/Ms _____

Address _____

City/State _____ Zip _____

Please allow four to six weeks for delivery.
Prices and availability subject to change without notice.   SC35-4/94